CRITICAL PERSPECTIVES ON
CYBERWARFARE

ANALYZING THE ISSUES

CRITICAL PERSPECTIVES ON CYBERWARFARE

Edited by Jennifer Peters

Enslow Publishing
101 W. 23rd Street
Suite 240
New York, NY 10011
USA

Published in 2019 by Enslow Publishing, LLC
101 W. 23rd Street, Suite 240, New York, NY 10011

Copyright © 2019 by Enslow Publishing, LLC

All rights reserved.

No part of this book may be reproduced by any means without the written permission of the publisher.

Library of Congress Cataloging-in-Publication Data

Names: Peters, Jennifer, editor.
Title: Critical perspectives on cyberwarfare / Jennifer Peters.
Description: New York : Enslow Publishing, [2019] | Series: Analyzing the issues | Audience: Grades 7-12. | Includes bibliographical references and index.
Identifiers: LCCN 2018000686| ISBN 9780766098459 (library bound) | ISBN 9780766098466 (pbk.)
Subjects: LCSH: Cyberterrorism—Juvenile literature.
Classification: LCC HV6773.15.C97 P48 2018 | DDC 363.325—dc23
LC record available at https://lccn.loc.gov/2018000686

Printed in the United States of America

To Our Readers: We have done our best to make sure all website addresses in this book were active and appropriate when we went to press. However, the author and the publisher have no control over and assume no liability for the material available on those websites or on any websites they may link to. Any comments or suggestions can be sent by email to customerservice@enslow.com.

Excerpts and articles have been reproduced with the permission of the copyright holders.

Photo Credits: Cover, 400tmax/E+/Getty Images; cover and interior pages graphics Thaiview/Shutterstock.com (cover top, pp. 3, 6-7), gbreezy/Shutterstock.com (magnifying glass), Ghornstern/Shutterstock.com (interior pages).

CONTENTS

INTRODUCTION 6

CHAPTER 1
WHAT THE EXPERTS SAY 8

CHAPTER 2
WHAT THE GOVERNMENT AND POLITICIANS SAY 54

CHAPTER 3
WHAT THE COURTS SAY 102

CHAPTER 4
WHAT ADVOCACY ORGANIZATIONS SAY 132

CHAPTER 5
WHAT THE MEDIA SAY 152

CHAPTER 6
WHAT ORDINARY PEOPLE SAY 182

CONCLUSION 209

BIBLIOGRAPHY 210
CHAPTER NOTES 213
GLOSSARY 217
FOR MORE INFORMATION 219
INDEX 221
ABOUT THE EDITOR 223

INTRODUCTION

In the twenty-first century, war doesn't only happen on battlefields, and the fighters aren't just men and women with guns. These days, warfare happens most often on the internet, with countries attacking each other through computers. Emails are hacked, diplomatic cables are leaked, and phones are tapped every day.

In 2016, the US media announced that Russia had declared war on the United States—but it wasn't a Cold War like in the 1980s, or a war like the US was fighting in Syria, Iraq, and Afghanistan. No, this war was taking place entirely online, and the actors involved weren't using guns, bombs, or even spies, at least not in the traditional sense. Instead, Russia was going to war with the United States online. They were hacking, eavesdropping, and interfering with the American presidential election without their agents ever having to leave their desks.

A few years earlier, North Korea attacked the United States—sort of. Instead of launching a nuclear missile or attacking US ships in the Pacific Ocean, North Korea hacked into the computer network of Sony, an American entertainment company, and leaked thousands of private emails, texts, and even advance copies of movies. They did this, they said, because they were upset over a movie Sony had produced that mocked North Korea's Supreme Leader, Kim Jong-Un. Already in a stand-off with America, North Korea felt the slight by Sony wasn't simply entertainment, but an attack by their Western enemy, so they chose to fight back.

America isn't just a victim of cyberattacks. American intelligence agencies use their own cyber tactics to fight enemies and protect their interests. From using new technology to hack into enemy missiles and tanks to spying on foreign leaders in order to make sure they always know what's going on, American military members are using all the tools at their disposal to make sure they can fight off the enemy no matter where they find them—whether that's on a battlefield or in the internet cables that run across the bottom of the Atlantic Ocean.

As technology becomes an even bigger part of our everyday lives, it will become a bigger part of how we fight wars, too. And that means American soldiers and intelligence agents will need to know how to fight battles both physical and digital.

That's why it's so important to explore all the ways modern technology and the internet have changed warfare in the twenty-first century, and the ways it will continue to change the wars we fight in the future.

CHAPTER 1

WHAT THE EXPERTS SAY

Cyberwarfare is still fairly new, but experts have been discussing it for years, ever since the internet became an everyday tool for military and defense workers. In the 1980s, cyberwarfare was considered enough of a reality to be used as the basis of a movie, *War Games*. More than three decades later, we're still debating the reality of cyberwar. Some say we're in the middle of a war right now, while others suggest that a cyberwar is coming but is not yet here. Some say cyberwar involves drones and electronic weapons, while others insist it is only cyberwar if the entire battle takes place in the wires that make up the worldwide web. In this chapter, you'll read articles by experts and academics that discuss just how real cyberwar is, and what constitutes cyberwar.

WHAT THE EXPERTS SAY

"CYBERWAR IS HERE TO STAY," BY PAUL ROSENZWEIG, FROM *THE CONVERSATION*, FEBRUARY 24, 2016

Last week, *The New York Times* revealed that the Obama administration had prepared a cyberattack plan to be carried out against Iran in the event diplomatic negotiations failed to limit that country's nuclear weapons development.

The plan, code-named Nitro Zeus, was said to be capable of disabling Iran's air defenses, communications system and parts of its electric grid. It also included an option to introduce a computer worm into the Iranian uranium enrichment facility at Fordow, to disrupt the creation of nuclear weapons. In anticipation of the need, U.S. Cyber Command placed hidden computer code in Iranian computer networks. According to *The New York Times*, President Obama saw Nitro Zeus as an option for confronting Iran that was "short of a full-scale war."

The reports, if true (to be fair, they have not been confirmed by any official sources), reflect a growing trend in the use of computers and networks to conduct military activity.

The United States is not, of course, the only practitioner. One notable example from recent history involves the apparent Russian assault on the transportation and electric grid in Ukraine. That attack, which happened late in 2015, was a "first of its kind" cyberassault that severely disrupted Ukraine's power system, affecting many innocent Ukrainian civilians. It bears noting that the vulnerabilities in Ukraine's power system are not unique – they exist in power grids across the globe, including the U.S. power grid and other major industrial facilities.

BUILT-IN VULNERABILITIES

The vulnerability of digital networks is, in many ways, an inevitable consequence of how the Internet was built. As then-Deputy Secretary of Defense William Lynn put it in a 2011 speech announcing our military strategy for operating in cyberspace: "The Internet was designed to be open, transparent and interoperable. Security and identity management were secondary objectives in system design. This lower emphasis on security in the internet's initial design … gives attackers a built-in advantage."

Among many factors, two in particular contribute to the growing sense of unease.

One is the problem of anonymity. Those who seek to do harm can easily do so at a distance, cloaked in the veil of anonymity behind false or shielded identities in the vastness of the web. With no built-in identity verification, pretending to be someone else is as easy as getting a new email address or registering a pseudonymous Facebook account.

Unmasking attackers is possible, but requires a significant investment of time and resources. It also often requires the "good guys" to use "bad guy" techniques to track the malefactors, because they need to hack the hackers to find out who they are. It took a Canadian company, using hacker techniques, more than a year to find out who had hacked the Dalai Lama's official computers – it was the Chinese.

In effect, this prevents targets from retaliating against attackers. Though most observers think Russia is behind the Ukrainian assault, there is no truly conclusive proof. It is very difficult to deter an unknown attacker. In addition, international coordination to respond to attacks

WHAT THE EXPERTS SAY

that threaten global stability can be stymied without solid proof of the source of an assault.

A NEW DEFINITION OF WAR

Second, and perhaps more significantly, the online world changes the boundaries of war. President Obama seems to think that cyberattacks are less than full-scale war (or so the *Times* reports). Is that realistic? Consider the following hypotheticals – all of which are reasonably plausible.

An adversary of the United States (known or unknown):
- Disrupts the stock exchanges for two days, preventing any trading;
- Uses a digital attack to take offline a radar system intended to provide early warning of an aerial attack on America;
- Steals the plans to the F-35 fighter;
- Disrupts the Pentagon's communication system;
- Introduces a latent piece of malware (a piece of malicious software that can be activated at a later date, sometimes called a "logic bomb") into a radar station that can disable the station when triggered, but doesn't trigger it just yet;
- Makes a nuclear centrifuge run poorly in a nuclear production plant, eventually causing physical damage to the centrifuge; or
- Implants a worm that slowly corrupts and degrades data on which certain military applications rely (such as GPS location data).

Some acts, like stealing the plans for a new fighter jet, won't be considered acts of war. Others, like disrupting our military command and control systems, look just like what we have always thought of as acts of war.

CRITICAL PERSPECTIVES ON CYBERWARFARE

INTRODUCING UNCERTAINTY

But what about the middle ground? Is leaving a logic bomb behind in a radar station like espionage, or is it similar to planting a mine in another country's harbor as a preparation for war? What about the computer code Nitro Zeus allegedly placed in the Iranian electric grid? And what if that code is still there?

These are hard questions. And they will endure. The very structures that make the Internet such a powerful engine for social activity and that have allowed its explosive, world-altering growth are also the factors that give rise to the vulnerabilities in the network. We could eliminate anonymity and restrict the potential for digital attacks, but only at the price of changing the ease with which peaceful people can use the Internet for novel commercial and social functions.

Those who want both ubiquity and security are asking to have their cake and eat it, too. So long as this Internet is "The Internet," vulnerability is here to stay. It can be managed, but it can't be eliminated. And that means that those who bear responsibility for defending the network have a persistent challenge of great complexity.

1. The author says that US president Barack Obama didn't consider a cyberattack to be a true act of war. Do you agree or disagree? Why?

WHAT THE EXPERTS SAY

2. Considering the possible outcomes of a cyber attack listed in the article, how serious should we consider these attacks? Is shutting down Ukraine's power grid less an act of war than bombing a city, if both result in the same outcome of loss of power?

"THE NEXT COLD WAR HAS ALREADY BEGUN—IN CYBERSPACE," BY CONOR DEANE-MCKENNA, FROM *THE CONVERSATION*, APRIL 7, 2016

The world is fighting a hidden war thanks to a massive shift in the technologies countries can use to attack each other. Much like the Cold War, the conflict is being fought indirectly rather than through open declarations of hostility. It has so far been fought without casualties but has the potential to cause suffering similar to that of any bomb blast. It is the Cyber War.

When we think of cyber attacks, we often think of terrorists or criminals hacking their way into our bank accounts or damaging government websites. But they have now been joined by agents of different governments that are launching cyber attacks against one another.

They aren't officially at war, but the tension between the US and Russia—and to a lesser degree China—remains high over a number of disputed decisions. Cyber attacks allow these countries to exert their power against each other in an often anonymous way. They can secretly make small gains but a wrong move could spell disaster, much like the operations of nuclear submarines during the Cold War.

There are numerous forms of cyber attacks that can be used. Malware, typically in the form of a Trojan horse or a worm, installs itself on a computer and takes control, often without the knowledge of the victim. Other attacks can disrupt computer systems through brute force. For example, distributed denial of service (DDOS) attacks involve flooding a system with so many requests to access a website that it crashes the site's server.

Countries are also trying to build up their cyber defences. Many infrastructural systems connected to power plants, for example, have been physically disconnected or "air-gapped" from the internet. Other defences such as firewalls and security programs are in place in all government systems to prevent their hacking by outside sources.

JUST AS DANGEROUS AS "REAL WAR"

Some argue that the idea of cyber warfare has been overhyped because cyber attacks don't have the physical consequences that "real" wars do. But the cyber weapons being used and developed could cause a large degree of economic as well as infrastructural damage – and this could endanger property and even human life. In 2007, scientists at the Idaho National Laboratory in the US were able to show how a cyber attack on an electricity generator could cause an explosion. This shows the real danger that cyber attacks can pose, not simply to national security infrastructure but also to hospitals, schools and homes.

WHAT THE EXPERTS SAY

The year 2007 was actually crucial in the history of cyber warfare, marking the point when several major states began putting cyber weapons to use in a well-documented way. After Estonia attempted to relocate a Soviet war memorial, Russia was accused of launching a series of DDOS attacks on Estonian websites including government and banking sites. Such action was not just embarrassing but damaging to both the power of the Estonian state and the economic activity of the country.

Although it wasn't discovered until 2010, the Stuxnet worm was the first prominent cyber weapon to be used by the US, and was originally deployed against Iran in 2007. The worm, part of the wider "Operation Olympic Games", was designed to prevent Iran from producing uranium that could be used in nuclear weapons. The software was hidden on a USB stick and uploaded to the control systems of the enrichment plant, causing its centrifuges to operate outside of safe parameters and leading to a series of breakdowns.

The Israeli cyber section, Unit 8200, which had a hand in the Stuxnet design, was also involved in the blackout of air radar during an attack on nuclear facilities in Syria in Operation Orchard, 2007. Shutting down the ageing Soviet-era radar through a mixture of cyber attacks allowed Israeli jets to bomb the site in the Deir-ez-Zor region of Syria.

The Israeli example shows how cyber attacks will start to become part of standard military operations. Both the US and Chinese cyber warfare divisions are parts of the countries' conventional military structures. And both states have made it clear that they will not rule out using cyber attacks for the sake of maintaining national security interests.

ACTING WITH IMPUNITY

These capabilities pose a danger to everyone, not just governments, and not just because they could lead to infrastructure being blown up. Stuxnet was discovered because the worm found its way onto the global internet and caused problems for tens of thousands of PCs across the world. It's not hard to imagine the widespread economic and personal damage that could be done with an even more malicious program. Stuxnet also shows why simply keeping critical infrastructure disconnected from the internet is not enough to protect it.

The other particularly worrying aspect of cyber warfare is that it allows states to act with relative impunity. Advanced encryption technologies make it almost impossible to prove exactly who is responsible for a specific cyber attack. As a result, states can now act unilaterally with little fear of open retaliation. For example, despite a bilateral agreement between the US and China to refrain from hacking for economic benefit, Chinese hackers have continued to infiltrate secure systems in the United States. There are few real consequences for this outright breach of sovereignty.

On the positive side, some have argued that cyber attacks allow states to pursue their foreign policy goals without using conventional military action, and could even dissuade superpowers from doing so. Disabling Iran's nuclear programme, for example, reduced the short-term likelihood the US would feel the need to make a military attack on the country. With tensions between superpowers high, but the risk of full-scale world war still relatively low, cyber attacks are likely to become an increasingly common way for countries to gain at their competitors' expense.

WHAT THE EXPERTS SAY

1. Issues of cyberwar affect not only countries' militaries, but civilian populations as well. After reading this article, how big of a risk do you think cyberattacks are to your daily life?

2. This article and the previous one mention electrical grids as prime targets for cyberattacks. What are some issues that you can foresee if a major American city lost power because of an attack?

"IS IT TIME FOR A CYBER PEACE CORPS?" BY SCOTT SHACKELFORD, FROM *THE CONVERSATION*, OCTOBER 25, 2017

Hackers around the world are attacking targets as diverse as North Dakota's state government, the Ukrainian postal service and a hospital in Jakarta, Indonesia. Unfortunately, many governments – in the developing world, and even cash-strapped states and local communities in the United States – lack the skills to effectively protect themselves.

The U.S. has an opportunity to serve itself and the world by revitalizing the ideals of global service popularized in another era of its history. Congress should expand the mandates of the Peace Corps and AmeriCorps to create a Cyber Peace Corps. It could do this by amending the Edward M. Kennedy Serve America Act, which was passed in 2009 to reorganize and expand the AmeriCorps program.

A CALL TO SERVICE

President John F. Kennedy established the Peace Corps in 1961 as a way for American volunteers to bring their skills and energy to the world. In the decades since, more than 225,000 Americans have served in the Peace Corps in more than 140 nations. Currently, there are more than 7,000 volunteers serving abroad in 65 nations working on a wide range of projects including fighting hunger by reducing soil erosion, promoting maternal health and teaching environmental sustainability.

Though not without its critics, overall the Peace Corps has done a tremendous amount of good around the world. It has long enjoyed strong bipartisan support at a relatively small cost.

Similarly, more than 900,000 Americans have served in AmeriCorps since its founding in 1993, at more than 21,000 locations across the country, contributing some 1.2 billion hours of service. These efforts are focused on community support in the U.S., through disaster response and recovery work, and providing assistance to local residents who are disabled, poor, elderly or homeless.

AmeriCorps has not enjoyed the same level of bipartisan political support as the Peace Corps, in part, some argue, because inadequate funding has limited its potential. The Serve America Act boosted AmeriCorps' funding to more than US$1 billion annually, for example, but this is an amount still far less than the $10 billion per year that the original proponents envisioned.

WHAT THE EXPERTS SAY

EXPANDING SERVICE OPTIONS

Adding cybersecurity to the mandates of America's national and international service programs would help fight the dire cyber-insecurity problems facing the country and the world. The effort could bolster political support, and funding, for the Peace Corps and AmeriCorps. But more importantly, it could help train the next generation of cybersecurity professionals.

Partnerships with universities and community colleges across the nation could create summer cybersecurity boot camps and clinics to teach young Americans how to defend computer systems against malicious hackers. That would help address the projected shortage of 1.8 million cybersecurity professionals by 2022, and prepare prospective members of a Cyber National Guard.

If Congress doesn't act, other options exist for both individuals and companies. A program like Teach for America could recruit willing volunteers and help prepare them for service. And private firms and civic groups could create their own coalitions, perhaps along the lines of the Service Corps of Retired Executives, linking trained professionals with communities needing help. A similar effort in India, the nonprofit Cyber Peace Foundation, has partnered cybersecurity experts with community organizations to help protect vulnerable populations, such as the elderly.

TOWARD CYBER PEACE

In the U.S., a pilot project could start with existing industry organizations focused on sharing cyber-threat information. Interested member corporations could contribute their workers for a fixed period of time to strengthen cybersecurity capabilities in their communities, including for school districts, municipalities and utility companies. Firms with international operations could do the same abroad.

When President Kennedy called for the creation of the Peace Corps during the turbulent 1960 election, the world was different: At the height of the Cold War, America faced a difficult challenge to win hearts and minds, especially in nations not yet aligned with either the U.S. or the Soviet Union. Today negative perceptions about the United States are rising around the world.

Developing U.S. cybersecurity talent and deploying it to mitigate threats to information security both at home and abroad would help protect vulnerable communities and rebuild social ties. In fact, the efforts involved in getting Cyber Peace Corps workers and their hosts to work together to protect potentially sensitive information may help strengthen trust and goodwill among nations. And it would recast 20th-century service commitments to face 21st-century challenges.

There are untold thousands of people on college campuses, working for small businesses and in leading tech firms who are worried about the world's lack of cybersecurity, but who feel powerless to change things. If given an opportunity, their work would help create the next generation of cybersecurity professionals. And it could offer new opportunities to bridge partisan divides at home, and geopolitical fault lines abroad.

WHAT THE EXPERTS SAY

1. What are ways that you can imagine helping the country through a cybersecurity Peace Corps?

2. Do you think America needs a cyber Peace Corps? Why or why not?

"IF TWO COUNTRIES WAGED CYBER WAR ON EACH ANOTHER, HERE'S WHAT TO EXPECT," BY BILL BUCHANAN, FROM *THE CONVERSATION*, AUGUST 5, 2016

Imagine you woke up to discover a massive cyber attack on your country. All government data has been destroyed, taking out healthcare records, birth certificates, social care records and so much more. The transport system isn't working, traffic lights are blank, immigration is in chaos and all tax records have disappeared. The internet has been reduced to an error message and daily life as you know it has halted.

This might sound fanciful but don't be so sure. When countries declare war on one another in future, this sort of disaster might be the opportunity the enemy is looking for. The internet has brought us many great things but it has made us more vulnerable. Protecting against such futuristic violence is one of the key challenges of the 21st century.

CRITICAL PERSPECTIVES ON CYBERWARFARE

Strategists know that the most fragile part of internet infrastructure is the energy supply. The starting point in serious cyber warfare may well be to trip the power stations which power the data centres involved with the core routing elements of the network.

Back-up generators and uninterruptible power supplies might offer protection, but they don't always work and can potentially be hacked. In any case, backup power is usually designed to shut off after a few hours. That is enough time to correct a normal fault, but cyber attacks might require backup for days or even weeks.

William Cohen, the former US secretary of defence, recently predicted such a major outage would cause large-scale economic damage and civil unrest throughout a country. In a war situation, this could be enough to bring about defeat. Janet Napolitano, a former secretary at the US Department of Homeland Security, believes the American system is not well enough protected to avoid this.

DENIAL OF SERVICE

An attack on the national grid could involve what is called a distributed denial of service (DDoS) attack. These use multiple computers to flood a system with information from many sources at the same time. This could make it easier for hackers to neutralise the backup power and tripping the system.

DDoS attacks are also a major threat in their own right. They could overload the main network gateways of a country and cause major outages. Such attacks are commonplace against the private sector, particularly finance companies. Akamai Technologies, which

WHAT THE EXPERTS SAY

controls 30% of internet traffic, recently said these are the most worrying kind of attack and becoming ever more sophisticated.

Akamai recently monitored a sustained attack against a media outlet of 363 gigabits per second (Gbps)—a scale which few companies, let alone a nation, could cope with for long. Networks specialist Verisign reports a shocking 111% increase in DDoS attacks per year, almost half of them over 10 Gbps in scale—much more powerful than previously. The top sources are Vietnam, Brazil and Colombia.

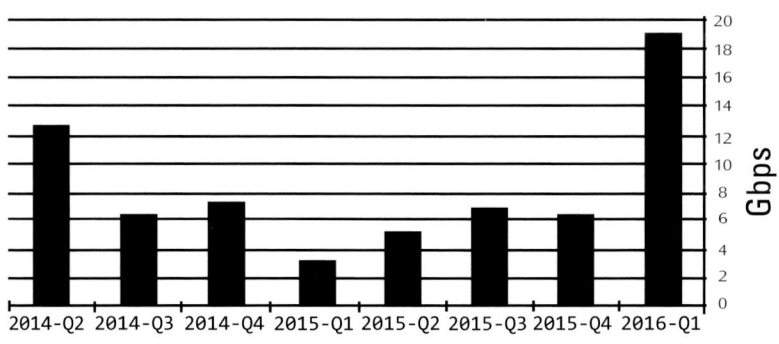

NUMBER OF ATTACKS

SCALE OF ATTACKS

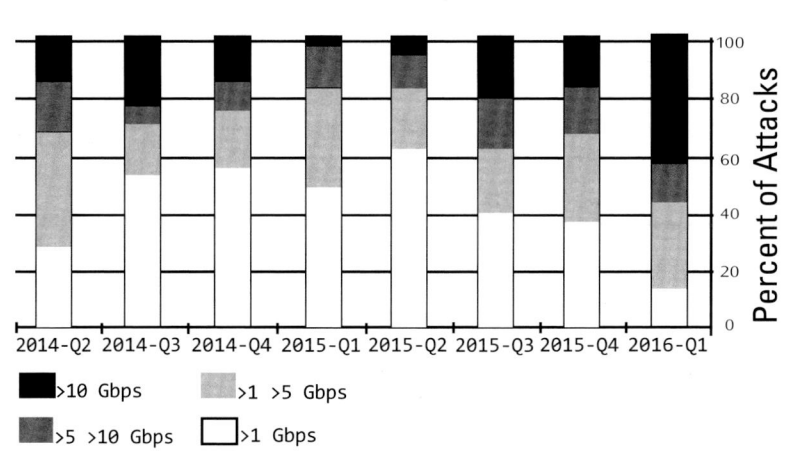

- >10 Gbps
- >1 >5 Gbps
- >5 >10 Gbps
- >1 Gbps

23

Most DDoS attacks swamp an internal network with traffic via the DNS and NTP servers that provide most core services within the network. Without DNS the internet wouldn't work, but it is weak from a security point of view. Specialists have been trying to come up with a solution, but building security into these servers to recognise DDoS attacks appears to mean re-engineering the entire internet.

HOW TO REACT

If a country's grid were taken down by an attack for any length of time, the ensuing chaos would potentially be enough to win a war outright. If instead its online infrastructure were substantially compromised by a DDoS attack, the response would probably go like this:

Phase one: Takeover of network: the country's security operations centre would need to take control of internet traffic to stop its citizens from crashing the internal infrastructure. We possibly saw this in the failed Turkish coup a few weeks ago, where YouTube and social media went completely offline inside the country.

Phase two: Analysis of attack: security analysts would be trying to figure out how to cope with the attack without affecting the internal operation of the network.

Phase three: Observation and large-scale control: the authorities would be faced with countless alerts about system crashes and problems. The challenge would be to ensure only key alerts reached the analysts trying to overcome the problems before

WHAT THE EXPERTS SAY

the infrastructure collapsed. A key focus would be ensuring military, transport, energy, health and law enforcement systems were given the highest priority, along with financial systems.

Phase four: Observation and fine control: by this stage there would be some stability and the attention could turn to lesser but important alerts regarding things like financial and commercial interests.

Phase five: Coping and restoring: this would be about restoring normality and trying to recover damaged systems. The challenge would be to reach this phase as quickly as possible with the least sustained damage.

STATE OF PLAY

If even the security-heavy US is concerned about its grid, the same is likely to be true of most countries. I suspect many countries are not well drilled to cope with sustained DDoS, especially given the fundamental weaknesses in DNS servers. Small countries are particularly at risk because they often depend on infrastructure that reaches a central point in a larger country nearby.

The UK, it should be said, is probably better placed than some countries to survive cyber warfare. It enjoys an independent grid and GCHQ and the National Crime Agency have helped to encourage some of the best private sector security operations centres in the world. Many countries could probably learn a great deal from it. Estonia, whose infrastructure was disabled for several days in 2007 following a cyber attack, is now looking at moving copies of government data to the UK for protection.

Given the current level of international tension and the potential damage from a major cyber attack, this is an area that all countries need to take very seriously. Better to do it now rather than waiting until one country pays the price. For better and worse, the world has never been so connected.

1. If a cyberattack brought down the internet or power grid, the author says chaos would ensue: traffic lights wouldn't work, important power systems at hospitals would go down, and it would be impossible to control entry and exits through US borders. Do you think this is more serious or less serious than if a military bombed a city? Explain.

"IN CYBER-WAR, YOU COULD CHANGE HISTORY AT THE TOUCH OF A BUTTON," BY DANIEL PRINCE AND MARK LACY, FROM *THE CONVERSATION*, MARCH 6, 2014

Not all violence in war and conflict is simply strategic. And not all the destruction that takes place is a consequence of territorial or geopolitical objectives. Taking over the next village, blocking a trade route or destroying the critical infrastructure that supports everyday life are the fundamentals of strategic advance but other actions are intended to undermine morale and have a psychological impact on the victim.

The degradation of the urban environment, or urbicide, is one such action. This is the destruction or desecration of buildings, the eradication of public space, the attempt to erase history and memory through attacks on libraries and sites of historical importance.

Urbicide is not just about physically removing people from a territory, it is an attempt to erase any trace of their existence in that territory. It is rewriting the history books to justify one side of an argument. This is particularly true for religious or ethnic conflicts, where one side aims to undermine the other's right to a disputed piece of land.

Cybercide, the cyber-crime equivilent to this practice, is a relatively new concept but could prove to be an equally powerful tool as we become more dependent on digital services in our daily lives. Yet we rarely think of preparing to defend ourselves against attack in this way.

DIGITAL DISRUPTION

Acts of cyber-vandalism are increasingly common and are used to deliver a message. They are symbolic statements that are often used to great effect.

Over a three-week period in April 2007, websites in Estonia were hit by denial of service attacks – a well known technique that aims to debilitate an online service by disrupting the technology on which it runs, such as internet connectivity. The websites of the Estonian parliament, banks and news outlets were hit, disrupting services for people across the country.

The attacks were a response to tensions between the Estonian government and Russian groups over the relocation of the Bronze Soldier of Tallin and other issues related to Soviet-era war graves.

Estonia's decision to move the statue away from Soviet war graves to the Tallinn Military Cemetery was seen by many as an act of traditional urbicide. The removal of the statue undermined the significance of the war grave sites and could make it easier to suggest they were never there. The denial-of-service attacks – for which a Russian official was later convicted – were an act of digital disruption. It was about attacking Estonian infrastructure and creating a nuisance in a time when people increasingly rely on websites in their everyday lives.

In another example, the Bangladeshi Cyber Army claimed that it had defaced around 1,000 websites in protest against the actions of India's Border Security Force. The attacks began on 7 January 2013, marking the two-year anniversary of the death of a 15-year-old Bangladeshi girl at the Indian border.

THE ROAD TO CYBERCIDE

Incidents like these are not full-blown cases of cybercide but they could well be seen as a sign of things to come. The attacks in Estonia and India were a nuisance but caused only temporary problems that could be resolved. The desecration of websites is more like digital graffiti, a means for those on the margins to circulate messages in public space and leave their mark. These acts may cause offence but there is no obvious permanent damage caused so they are not the same as destroying a bridge or

WHAT THE EXPERTS SAY

a building. Only those unwary website owners who don't back up their online content suffer long-term problems when attacked in this way.

Cyberspace is fast becoming fundamental to life. The web is now vital for commerce and more aspects of our lives are stored and shaped through digital culture than ever before. It's possible that attacks like those carried out in Estonia or India or by the Syrian Electronic Army could be more permanent and severe.

In the race to digitize more and more aspects of our existence we might be failing to grasp the potential accidents and vulnerabilities on the horizon. The speed and efficiency with which we try to digitize services might limit thinking and planning on the more negative unintended consequences of technological change.

How safe are our financial details, for example? Would a group be able to delete our financial histories or – in conjunction with ethnic cleansing – erase property deeds to make it seem like certain people have no rights on land?

And what of libraries and artefacts? More and more books and music are being published digitally – sometimes with a hard copy version but sometimes without. If, in 30 years time, we find ourselves in the age of completely digital libraries, a whole new set of vulnerabilities is possible.

In 2009, Kindle owners who had bought the George Orwell classic *1984* woke up one day to find Amazon had simply erased the title from their devices. Hard copies still exist, of course, but which future classics do or will only exist in digital form in the future? A decision such as this by a company or a government could wipe that piece of literature off the face of the Earth. Just as Stalin used what technology was available to him in his time to repaint history, the dictators of the future might try to re-write history by altering the books stored in online national libraries.

Of course, it can be argued that the "distributed" nature of digital life provides protection. Information is distributed across too many locations to be completely erased, which protects us from the actions of states or criminal organisations that would seek to control information. Anxiety about future cybercide may well be a symptom of living in a time of rapid and disruptive social, economic and political change but that doesn't mean we shouldn't plan for the future.

However, cybercide potentially embodies more subtle forms of social manipulation. It is relatively hard to degrade or alter the urban environment to erase a group of people or a historical artifact without anyone noticing. And yet the subversion and subtle manipulation of digitally held information is the lifeblood of hackers the world over.

What if the aim is not to destroy a whole piece of literature, but to subtly alter the text, say of a school book to change its meaning or remove passages from disputed literature. These changes may not be noticed in time to prevent them from becoming conventional wisdom or perception. They could change a whole generation's understanding of a historic event or specific social group.

The concept of cybercide provides an infinite spectrum of disruptive possibilities to undermine morale and have a psychological impact on the intended victims. Ones that may be more subtle and seditious than we have seen before or could possibly imagine.

WHAT THE EXPERTS SAY

1. So many things we own are digital today: books, music, movies, important documents, family photos, and videos. What are some ways that these things can be used against us in a cyberattack?

2. The author mentions more subtle cyberattacks, like changing the text of e-books to rewrite history or erasing news. What other subtle ways might you forsee an attacker using technology?

"STRUGGLING WITH CYBER: A CRITICAL LOOK AT WAGING WAR ONLINE," BY DANIEL MOORE, FROM *WAR ON THE ROCKS*, JULY 5, 2017

If media coverage is to be believed, we are in the midst of a cyberwar with daily attacks occurring across several theaters. Between dropping "cyber-bombs" on the Islamic State, Chinese intruders pilfering precious technology, and Russian information operations shaping the U.S. political process, it seems that the continuous power struggle between nations is now most commonly waged on the internet. While there might be some truth to that narrative, the reality is — of course — more nuanced. It's difficult to define and explain attacks that are entirely virtual. To understand this, one must understand a few points about offensive network operations. First, cyber operations are not as novel as they appear. Rather, they draw heavily from the integration of electronic warfare into joint operations. Second, different nations have largely different perspectives on how to employ network capabilities to achieve political objectives. Third, most incidents we label as "cyberattacks" or "cyber warfare" do not in fact merit being called such.

CYBER EVOLUTION

The United States and NATO have declared networks to be a fifth domain of warfare, cementing the perception that it is novel and distinct. We have also seen massive investments and doctrinal updates towards cyber-related activities. But network operations are neither entirely novel nor do they necessarily constitute warfare. Perhaps then we should stop automatically defining them as such. Labeling an incident an "attack" can have tremendous consequences, especially when carried out by one nation against another. Indeed, NATO's secretary general just revealed that that alliance's leaders "decided that a cyberattack can trigger Article 5." It is therefore crucial that everyone from the world leader to the average citizen have an informed understanding of what exactly constitutes an "attack."

Offensive network operations — essentially military cyber-attacks — are a combination of information operations, intelligence collection, and electronic warfare. As such, they draw familiar characteristics from each of these, creating a unique but not altogether new activity. Much like their electronic predecessors, offensive network operations target the trust between operators and equipment. They

WHAT THE EXPERTS SAY

do this by influencing the flow and presentation of data. If operators can't rely on their sensors, communication links, or autonomous platforms, they are not left with much else. Rather than physically targeting human beings or equipment, network operations can qualify as attacks when they seek to degrade, disrupt, or destroy software and networks.

Let's turn to a classic example of electronic warfare: targeting radars to cripple anti-air defenses. This is traditionally done either by either flooding the radar image with false matches, interfering with the transmission itself, or influencing the radar waves returned by a hostile aircraft so it appears as something else. These are essentially all external means of making the radar less functional.

A modern network attack on the same air defense network may instead use internal means. By penetrating the air defense network, an adversary may alter the inner workings of the network's radars or targeting systems. Friendly aircraft could be recoded as hostile aircraft and vice versa, or altogether wiped off the radar image. Targeting coordinates might be altered so that any missiles launched would hit empty space. Those are only a few of the possibilities for a nuanced but significant operation against an air defense system.

The myth of the high-impact high-availability cyberattack is pervasive but ultimately difficult to implement at scale. As with their predecessors in electronic warfare, network operations are voracious consumers of accurate intelligence. It is impossible to conduct high-quality, impactful offensive network operations without first gaining in-depth familiarity with the specific target. In most cases, in order to shut down military equipment by way of a cyberattack, an attacker would need to (a) obtain access to the platform or network, (b) analyze the system for specific vulnerabilities, (c) weaponize an exploit capable of achieving the operational goal, (d) maintain a covert foothold in the network until the attack is needed, and, finally, (e) successfully execute the attack and perform a bomb damage assessment — the digital equivalent of observing the impact of an armed attack on a target. This process will not only vary per type of military hardware, but potentially even per different deployments of the same hardware. Even the same equipment deployed in other scenarios and configurations might call for a new operation.

Cyber capabilities that work "out of the box" often provide little more than good tactical value. In a recent publication, the U.S. Army detailed how its fire teams utilize cyber capabilities against the Islamic State's communication networks used by the Islamic State in the field. Much like classic jamming, Army operators attack the communication network itself rather than its electromagnetic transmissions. Network operations are therefore often viewed as a component of joint operations, contributing to warfighting efforts by supporting other domains and reducing adversary capability to do the same. They do not include all adversarial interactions in cyberspace.

DIFFERING PERSPECTIVES

The West does not hold monopoly over all matters cyber, but it does seem to have a monopoly on its obsession with the terminology. While Western audiences obsess about "cyberattacks" and "cyberwar," other nations have been

WHAT THE EXPERTS SAY

busily integrating network operations into their doctrine in unique ways. Different approaches to targeting networks represent varying requirements and doctrine. Where China might use network operations to offset conventional superiority of a highly connected force such as that of the U.S. military, Israel might view network operations as a set of tools that enable stealthier, less violent strikes.

Russia has an elaborate history of maneuvering to influence the flow and shape of information. However, it has no independent concept of "cyber warfare." The Russian transliteration of the term (kibervoyna) is primarily used when discussing Western approaches to network operations. Instead, Russian military doctrine and official literature as analyzed by experts portray network attacks holistically, as another toolset used both in peace and wartime to help facilitate political success. In this sense, cyberattacks are a specific set of capabilities on an expansive information operations spectrum. There are ample examples to perfectly encapsulate different facets of this approach. An earlier case is the 2007 Estonia incident, when the removal of a Soviet-era war memorial from a Tallinn square triggered a barrage of denial of service attacks against Estonian websites, ostensibly facilitated by Russia to signal its political displeasure. While the attack had minimal lasting effect or political value, it was heard loudly and clearly in Estonia and the rest of NATO. Both quickly proceeded to establish NATO's Cooperative Cyber Defense Center of Excellence in Tallinn.

The breach of the U.S. Democratic National Committee in 2016 and the clumsy but effective disinformation campaign that followed was an unprecedented breach of sovereignty perpetrated through a network intrusion. It embodied the Russian approach to information operations, which view them in part as a means of beneficially shaping the political landscape in peacetime, thereby creating more favorable outcomes befitting Russian grand strategy. In this sense, while the operation was not an attack or cyberwar by any meaningful metric, it indicated the type of operations for which network intrusions are often more suitable for when used strategically to pursue political objectives.

There are other operational Russian examples that show the usefulness of cyberattacks in political signaling. In December 2015, a portion of the Ukrainian power grid suffered several hours of outage. Ukrainian authorities quickly identified it as a Russian-perpetrated network attack. It caused minimal lasting damage and had dubious impact in the ongoing war in the country's east, but it at the very least sent an unmistakable message: If conflict escalates, attacks against critical infrastructure are both on the table and within Moscow's technical and operational reach. While we have no visibility into political messaging that may have accompanied the operation, it perhaps was an attempt at political coercion or deterrence by way of cyberattack.

A controversial report by the U.S. information security company CrowdStrike suggests that Russia also relies on cyber operations for direct battlefield assistance. A network operation tied to Russian intelligence by technical indicators successfully targeted a mobile phone application supposedly used by Ukrainian military forces to calculate and direct fire for a specific type of artillery. If the details are even partially true, it suggests that a network operation directly contributed to physically targeting military hardware. However, as the operation was only used to collect intelligence on artillery locations rather than tamper with guidance calculation, the operation would again fall more within the bounds of an intelligence maneuver than an actual attack. If the operation had also covertly altered the targeting information as to impact the accuracy of Ukrainian artillery fire, that could have constituted a cyber-attack.

Alternatively, Chinese doctrine has gradually cemented the role of network operations as a key component in shattering conventional asymmetries. This approach permeates beyond the battlefield to economic and political agendas. Operations to illicitly acquire intellectual property can allow getting access to cutting edge technologies instead of expensively developing or purchasing them, thereby subverting the need for long and costly research processes. At the same time, vast outfits of indeterminably-affiliated online users identify potential online political hotspots and troll via commentary to skew public opinion. Other units attempt to infiltrate adversary military networks to preposition for possible wartime efforts.

After the first Gulf War, the People's Liberation Army identified the unmistakable reality of the modern U.S. doctrine. It was made glaringly obvious that integrating joint warfare based on an unprecedented flow of networked sensory data allowed effective direction of resources and combat operations. Simultaneously, networked joint warfare created new so-called centers of gravity. The dependence of American forces on continuous data means if one can reduce the availability of that data or corrupt it, one can severely impact U.S. military operations. Those writing Chinese military doctrine gradually responded, with increasing references to network attacks designed to hinder forward-deployed

U.S. regional forces. If the Chinese military sought to move against Taiwan or targets in the South China Sea, targeting U.S. forces through cyberspace could presumably slow their ability to muster an effective response to defend an ally. China could do this by tampering with logistical data, undermining sensors, or disrupting communication.

EXCLUDING FOR CLARITY

An intelligence operation — no matter how successful — is not intrinsically an armed attack. When intruders breached the U.S. Office of Personnel Management in 2015 and made off with an exorbitant amount of sensitive information, some in the government elected to label the intrusion an attack on U.S. infrastructure. By contrast, the Chinese government — which was, according to Washington, responsible for the operation — quickly labeled the theft as a criminal incident and even claimed to arrest the perpetrators. Aside from sharp rhetoric, the United States had precious little recourse available that would not be disproportionately escalatory. The reason for this was simple: While undoubtedly an embarrassing loss of important, the OPM breach was by no means an attack. Valuable intelligence was stolen, but no system or network was impacted in any way.

Influence campaigns also do not automatically merit being called attacks. At times, nations seeking to change the political climate of other countries would seek to do so by trying to covertly shape public discourse and sharing of information. This particular brand of information operations is practiced by many nations and often referred to as "active measures" when wielded by Russia. Perhaps the most notable such case was the

WHAT THE EXPERTS SAY

alleged intervention of Russian intelligence agencies in the contentious 2016 U.S. election process. The hack into the Democratic National Committee turned into an awkwardly spun web of disinformation seemingly intent on discrediting the Clinton-led Democratic campaign. Even a brazen operation that constituted a meaningful breach of national sovereignty did not eventually qualify as an actual attack by Russia on the United States. Could it have triggered hostilities between Russia and the United States under different circumstances? Perhaps. It was, after all, a blatant political intervention. Ironically, even official Russian doctrine specifically lists significant breaches of political sovereignty as one of its top military threats:

> Use of information and communication technologies for the military-political purposes to take actions which run counter to international law, being aimed against sovereignty, political independence, territorial integrity of states and posing threat to the international peace, security, global and regional stability.

But despite its significance, the operation against the Democratic National Convention did not truly qualify as network-enabled violence on its own. While documents were perhaps tampered with for political effect, no system, network, or platform were directly degraded or manipulated in the operation. As then-Director of National Intelligence Clapper confirmed, it was an aggressive influence operation, it was a successful espionage campaign, but it wasn't a cyberattack.

Lastly, intrusions and theft perpetrated for a financial motive — especially but not exclusively when carried out by criminal groups — are neither attacks nor do they constitute cyberwar. Even if a skilled malware group with possible links to the Russian government exclusively targets customers of Western banks, it does not indicate political will or a military circumstance. Similarly, a national effort by North Korea to target the SWIFT financial network in an elaborate network operation to steal vast amounts of money does not inherently mean it is an attack. Were the intruders to cripple SWIFT networks just as North Korean intruders previously targeted Sony, rather than just a theft of money, that could arguably be framed as an attack on the global financial order. Instead, it was an elaborate and illegal operation certainly in breach of international norms but otherwise non-violent in nature. The operation was just a modern, networked version of criminal activities North Korea routinely undertakes to subvert crippling sanctions — a cyber-enabled bank robbery.

FOCUSING ON REALITY

It's crucial to pinpoint what cyber warfare actually means. Definitions inform perception and discussion, which in turn affects the shaping of public policy. If all manners of network intrusions continue to be labeled as cyberattacks — or, worse, as warfare — the discussion around actual offensive network operation suffers immeasurably. Intelligence operations are not comfortably on the spectrum of war. Nor is crime. Nor are peacetime influence operations, as wildly successful and sovereignty-breaching as they may be. Taking the notion that intelligence operations constitute attacks risks further increasing already rising global tension levels. If an operation is perceived as an attack, the victim is then expected to respond with the toolset reserved for confronting attacks. Instead, intelligence campaigns are accepted as commonplace between rivals and allies alike. Victims may attempt to mitigate, pursue counter-measures, or even deter, but the playing field is decidedly calmer than that of the battlefield.

There are still plenty of visible instances in which network operations are integrated into actual military doctrine across all levels of warfare. From assisting combatants in degrading enemy communication infrastructure to disabling air defense networks, the potential for meaningful integration of network operations into joint doctrine is immense. For tactical value, these operations require extensive research and development to identify vulnerabilities in targeted adversary military hardware. For strategic operations, attacks must be predicated by elaborate peacetime intelligence operations designed to acquire access to the sensitive systems later targeted in conflict. This means that the more comprehensive and impactful the network attack seeks to be, the more prepositioning and accurate, consistent intelligence is required to enable success.

It is more constructive to view "cyber warfare" as offensive network operations aimed at attaining military objectives. This is a thoroughly restrictive definition excluding the overwhelming majority of intrusions reported on daily, but it is meant to be so. It still leaves a wide range of possibilities, from the most tactical attacks against a local communication grid to operational attacks against defensive hardware, costly strategic operations meant to cripple joint warfare throughout a theatre, and even attacks against critical infrastructure to weaken populace resolve. Different capabilities and resources characterizes each tier of operations, but they all reliably fall within the military gamut.

When next confronted with a network intrusion characterized as an attack, it is important to ask who was targeted and how were they impacted? If it's written up or described as cyber warfare, it is even more important to ask; who was involved on both sides? Was there a discernible military-political objective? Were victim assets degraded, disrupted, or destroyed in any meaningful way? Applying these simple questions to most of what is commonly labelled as cyber warfare will immediately exclude almost all such cases. That's for the better.

1. The author discusses how not all cyberattacks are equal: some should be considered acts of war, while others are less serious. Based on the argument he makes, and what you've read so far, where would you draw the line between cyberwar and a less serious cyberattack?

2. When a cyber intrusion is made for financial means, the author says it is not an attack or an act of war. Do you agree? List three reasons why or why not.

"READY, AIM, CLICK: WE NEED NEW LAWS TO GOVERN CYBERWARFARE," BY BELA BONITA CHATTERJEE, FROM *THE CONVERSATION*, AUGUST 21, 2014

President Bush is reported to have said: "When I take action, I'm not going to fire a US$2m missile at a US$10 empty tent and hit a camel in the butt. It's going to be decisive." As the quote suggests, when it comes to national defence, enemies are unlikely to be deterred by an army of three, a leaky canoe and a fleet of second-hand microlights. In times of war we usually expect a powerful, graphic display of military might.

Nations may feel reassured that the sheer scale and sophistication of their armed forces will be enough to deter any potential threat, with would-be attackers put off by the mere prospect of retaliation. But what if decisive action can be conducted without armed forces, without firing a single bullet, but by simply pressing "enter"?

This is the promise of cyber-warfare, where the hostile use of software against a state's critical infrastructure such as energy and transport networks, financial markets, hospitals, can have immediate and devastating effects. The tools of cyber-warfare could be acquired with relative ease by new belligerent nations who were hitherto considered unthreatening by virtue of their lack of conventional forces. Belligerents may not even be nations, but unaffiliated hackers driven by a common political, religious or economic ideology, who can quickly form, strike and disperse using the anonymity of the internet to hide their tracks.

Nations have had to take the threat of cyber-warfare seriously. Several significant military powers have now publicly declared policies on cyber-warfare, and the topic has dominated diplomatic exchanges at the highest level. Perhaps the most poignant acknowledgement of cyber-warfare as a serious issue comes from its inclusion as a topic of importance in the 2011 Report of the International Red Cross on International Humanitarian Law and the challenges of contemporary armed conflicts.

The growing recognition of cyber-warfare as a topic of legal concern in particular is of great importance, particularly for international law, which, among other things, it sets out a framework for the legally permissible use of force. International Humanitarian Law (also known as the Law of Armed Conflict) is the part of international law which tries to ensure that if there is armed conflict, it is conducted in as humane and restrained a manner as possible.

Determining how legal rules apply to cyber-warfare is obviously important. States will want to know whether cyber-offensives will come under the rules of international law, what limits may be applied and what action can be taken in response within the law. If a cyber-war is unavoidable, then states will also want to know what rules apply to the actual conduct of such war, for example in determining what targets are permissible, how rules on neutrality apply, and what kinds of cyber-weapons are permissible.

However, there is a lack of clarity on how international law applies to cyber-warfare. International law has evolved over time and is heavily influenced by traditional concepts of conventional armed warfare between clearly defined nation states. Cyber-warfare is so new it is not specifically addressed in any treaties. It is difficult enough to reach an agreement on international matters at the best of times, especially in dealing with conflicts. This difficulty will undoubtedly apply to cyber-warfare too.

In light of this considerable uncertainty, a recent report for Security Lancaster outlines an agenda for future legal research on cyber-warfare. This calls for a reconsideration of whether international law is a useful framework. For example, international law focuses heavily on states, but are future cyber-attacks likely to come from states themselves? How should cyber-hostilities initiated by federated or balkanised hacker groups with no clear state affiliation be legally categorised? Would we be better off starting to construct a legal framework from scratch as opposed to one built around outdated concepts that no longer reflect the current military realities?

It should be acknowledged that not all share the view that cyber-warfare is a significant or worrying prospect. Its detractors point out that it has been responsible for no human casualties to date, and no hostile cyber-incident has as yet been treated as an act of war or openly admitted to by a state. But this ought not to deter us from taking the issue seriously, and to start thinking about an acceptable – and perhaps more importantly, workable – legal framework to cover the resort to and conduct of cyber-warfare.

We would do well to recall that another world leader, Winston Churchill, was widely derided at the time for forecasting the onset of World War II, and remember that if the lessons of history are not learned they are destined to be repeated. If World War III promises to be digital, we must be as prepared as we can be.

CRITICAL PERSPECTIVES ON CYBERWARFARE

1. As noted in this article, there are not many laws—national or international—guiding cyberwarfare. What do you think are some ground rules that should guide cyberattacks?

2. Some people consider cyberwar less serious because no one has been killed by cyberattacks. Do you agree with this? If this is the case, does that mean there is no need for laws governing cyberwar?

"HOW VULNERABLE TO HACKING IS THE US ELECTION CYBER INFRASTRUCTURE?" BY RICHARD FORNO, FROM *THE CONVERSATION*, JULY 29, 2016

Following the hack of Democratic National Committee emails and reports of a new cyberattack against the Democratic Congressional Campaign Committee, worries abound that foreign nations may be clandestinely involved in the 2016 American presidential campaign. Allegations swirl that Russia, under the direction of President Vladimir Putin, is secretly working to undermine the U.S. Democratic Party. The apparent logic is that a Donald Trump presidency would result in more pro-Russian policies. At the moment, the FBI is investigating, but no U.S. government agency has yet made a formal accusation.

WHAT THE EXPERTS SAY

The Republican nominee added unprecedented fuel to the fire by encouraging Russia to "find" and release Hillary Clinton's missing emails from her time as secretary of state. Trump's comments drew sharp rebuke from the media and politicians on all sides. Some suggested that by soliciting a foreign power to intervene in domestic politics, his musings bordered on criminality or treason. Trump backtracked, saying his comments were "sarcastic," implying they're not to be taken seriously.

Of course, the desire to interfere with another country's internal political processes is nothing new. Global powers routinely monitor their adversaries and, when deemed necessary, will try to clandestinely undermine or influence foreign domestic politics to their own benefit. For example, the Soviet Union's foreign intelligence service engaged in so-called "active measures" designed to influence Western opinion. Among other efforts, it spread conspiracy theories about government officials and fabricated documents intended to exploit the social tensions of the 1960s. Similarly, U.S. intelligence services have conducted their own secret activities against foreign political systems – perhaps most notably its repeated attempts to help overthrow pro-communist Fidel Castro in Cuba.

Although the Cold War is over, intelligence services around the world continue to monitor other countries' domestic political situations. Today's "influence operations" are generally subtle and strategic. Intelligence services clandestinely try to sway the "hearts and minds" of the target country's population toward a certain political outcome.

What has changed, however, is the ability of individuals, governments, militaries and criminal or terrorist organizations to use internet-based tools – commonly called cyberweapons – not only to gather information but also to generate influence within a target group.

So what are some of the technical vulnerabilities faced by nations during political elections, and what's really at stake when foreign powers meddle in domestic political processes?

VULNERABILITIES AT THE ELECTRONIC BALLOT BOX

The process of democratic voting requires a strong sense of trust – in the equipment, the process and the people involved.

One of the most obvious, direct ways to affect a country's election is to interfere with the way citizens actually cast votes. As the United States (and other nations) embrace electronic voting, it must take steps to ensure the security – and more importantly, the trustworthiness – of the systems. Not doing so can endanger a nation's domestic democratic will and create general political discord – a situation that can be exploited by an adversary for its own purposes.

As early as 1975, the U.S. government examined the idea of computerized voting, but electronic voting systems were not used until Georgia's 2002 state elections. Other states have adopted the technology since then, although given ongoing fiscal constraints, those with aging or problematic electronic voting machines are returning to more traditional (and cheaper) paper-based ones.

New technology always comes with some glitches – even when it's not being attacked.

WHAT THE EXPERTS SAY

For example, during the 2004 general election, North Carolina's Unilect e-voting machines "lost" 4,438 votes due to a system error.

But cybersecurity researchers focus on the kinds of problems that could be intentionally caused by bad actors. In 2006, Princeton computer science professor Ed Felten demonstrated how to install a self-propagating piece of vote-changing malware on Diebold e-voting systems in less than a minute. In 2011, technicians at the Argonne National Laboratory showed how to hack e-voting machines remotely and change voting data.

Voting officials recognize that these technologies are vulnerable. Following a 2007 study of her state's electronic voting systems, Ohio Secretary of State Jennifer L. Brunner announced that

> *the computer-based voting systems in use in Ohio do not meet computer industry security standards and are susceptible to breaches of security that may jeopardize the integrity of the voting process.*

As the first generation of voting machines ages, even maintenance and updating become an issue. A 2015 report found that electronic voting machines in 43 of 50 U.S. states are at least 10 years old — and that state election officials are unsure where the funding will come from to replace them.

SECURING THE MACHINES AND THEIR DATA

In many cases, electronic voting depends on a distributed network, just like the electrical grid or municipal water system. Its spread-out nature means there are many points of potential vulnerability.

First, to be secure, the hardware "internals" of each voting machine must be made tamper-proof at the point of manufacture. Each individual machine's software must remain tamper-proof and accountable, as must the vote data stored on it. (Some machines provide voters with a paper receipt of their votes, too.) When problems are discovered, the machines must be removed from service and fixed. Virginia did just this in 2015 once numerous glaring security vulnerabilities were discovered in its system.

Once votes are collected from individual machines, the compiled results must be transmitted from polling places to higher election offices for official consolidation, tabulation and final statewide reporting. So the network connections between locations must be tamper-proof and prevent interception or modification of the in-transit tallies. Likewise, state-level vote-tabulating systems must have trustworthy software that is both accountable and resistant to unauthorized data modification. Corrupting the integrity of data anywhere during this process, either intentionally or accidentally, can lead to botched election results.

However, technical vulnerabilities with the electoral process extend far beyond the voting machines at the "edge of the network." Voter registration and administration systems operated by state and national governments are at risk too. Hacks here could affect voter rosters and citizen databases. Failing to secure these systems and records could result in fraudulent information in the voter database that may lead to improper (or illegal) voter registrations and potentially the casting of fraudulent votes.

And of course, underlying all this is human vulnerability: Anyone involved with e-voting technologies or procedures is susceptible to coercion or human error.

WHAT THE EXPERTS SAY

HOW CAN WE GUARD THE SYSTEMS?

The first line of defense in protecting electronic voting technologies and information is common sense. Applying the best practices of cybersecurity, data protection, information access and other objectively developed, responsibly implemented procedures makes it more difficult for adversaries to conduct cyber mischief. These are essential and must be practiced regularly.

Sure, it's unlikely a single voting machine in a specific precinct in a specific polling place would be targeted by an overseas or criminal entity. But the security of each electronic voting machine is essential to ensuring not only free and fair elections but fostering citizen trust in such technologies and processes – think of the chaos around the infamous hanging chads during the contested 2000 Florida recount. Along these lines, in 2004, Nevada was the first state to mandate e-voting machines include a voter-verified paper trail to ensure public accountability for each vote cast.

Proactive examination and analysis of electronic voting machines and voter information systems are essential to ensuring free and fair elections and facilitating citizen trust in e-voting. Unfortunately, some voting machine manufacturers have invoked the controversial Digital Millennium Copyright Act to prohibit external researchers from assessing the security and trustworthiness of their systems.

However, a 2015 exception to the act authorizes security research into technologies otherwise protected by copyright laws. This means the security community can legally research, test, reverse-engineer and analyze such systems. Even more importantly, researchers now have the freedom to publish their findings without fear of being sued for copyright infringement. Their work is vital to identifying security vulnerabilities before they can be exploited in real-world elections.

Because of its benefits and conveniences, electronic voting may become the preferred mode for local and national elections. If so, officials must secure these systems and ensure they can provide trustworthy elections that support the democratic process. State-level election agencies must be given the financial resources to invest in up-to-date e-voting systems. They also must guarantee sufficient, proactive, ongoing and effective protections are in place to reduce the threat of not only operational glitches but intentional cyberattacks.

Democracies endure based not on the whims of a single ruler but the shared electoral responsibility of informed citizens who trust their government and its systems. That trust must not be broken by complacency, lack of resources or the intentional actions of a foreign power. As famed investor Warren Buffett once noted, "It takes 20 years to build a reputation and five minutes to ruin it."

In cyberspace, five minutes is an eternity.

1. Some allege that the 2016 US presidential election was hacked, and this article discusses the ways in which such a thing could occur. Based on what you've read, do you think an American presidential election can be hacked?

WHAT THE EXPERTS SAY

2. During the 2000 US presidential elections, there were problems with paper ballots in Florida. Meanwhile, this article discusses issues faced by electronic voting systems. Both systems, then, have problems. Based on this, and on what you've read, do you think that means we should avoid moving toward a fully digital voting system?

CHAPTER 2

WHAT THE GOVERNMENT AND POLITICIANS SAY

Politicians discuss cybersecurity issues every day, in speeches and in proposed legislation. But like the experts, there is no agreement yet on what constitutes cyberwar and how serious a cyber attack is compared to a more physical attack. The information on what kinds of attacks are even possible is still new, and with technology evolving every single day, it's hard for even the president to know what's possible and how serious it is. In the following articles and speeches, you'll see how different members of the federal government have responded to cyberwarfare issues in recent years and what their responses to the changing technological times mean for the future of cybersecurity.

WHAT THE GOVERNMENT AND POLITICIANS SAY

EXCERPT FROM "REMARKS BY THE PRESIDENT AT THE CYBERSECURITY AND CONSUMER PROTECTION SUMMIT," BY BARACK OBAMA, FROM THE WHITE HOUSE ARCHIVES, FEBRUARY 13, 2015

As we gather here today, America is seeing incredible progress that we can all be proud of. We just had the best year of job growth since the 1990s. (Applause.) Over the past 59 months, our businesses have created nearly 12 million new jobs, which is the longest streak of private sector job growth on record. And in a hopeful sign for middle-class families, wages are beginning to rise again.

And, meanwhile, we're doing more to prepare our young people for a competitive world. Our high school graduation rate has hit an all-time high. More Americans are finishing college than ever before. Here at Stanford and across the country, we've got the best universities, we've got the best scientists, the best researchers in the world. We've got the most dynamic economy in the world. And no place represents that better than this region. So make no mistake, more than any other nation on Earth, the United States is positioned to lead in the 21st century.

And so much of our economic competitiveness is tied to what brings me here today, and that is America's leadership in the digital economy. It's our ability -- almost unique across the planet -- our ability to innovate and to learn, and to discover, and to create, and build, and do business online, and stretch the boundaries of what's possible. That's what drives us. And so when we had to decide where to have this summit, the decision was easy,

CRITICAL PERSPECTIVES ON CYBERWARFARE

because so much of our Information Age began right here, at Stanford.

It was here where two students, Bill Hewlett and Dave Packard, met and then, in a garage not far from here, started a company that eventually built one of the first personal computers, weighing in at 40 pounds. (Laughter.) It was from here, in 1968, where a researcher, Douglas Englebart, astonished an audience with two computers, connected "online," and hypertext you could click on with something called a "mouse."

A year later, a computer here received the first message from another computer 350 miles away -- the beginnings of what would become the Internet. And, by the way, it's no secret that many of these innovations built on government-funded research is one of the reasons that if we want to maintain our economic leadership in the world, America has to keep investing in basic research in science and technology. It's absolutely critical. (Applause.)

So here at Stanford, pioneers developed the protocols and architecture of the Internet, DSL, the first webpage in America, innovations for cloud computing. Student projects here became Yahoo and Google. Those were pretty good student projects. (Laughter.) Your graduates have gone on to help create and build thousands of companies that have shaped our digital society -- from Cisco to Sun Microsystems, YouTube to Instagram, StubHub, Bonobos. According to one study, if all the companies traced back to Stanford graduates formed their own nation, you'd be one the largest economies in the world and have a pretty good football team as well. (Laughter and applause.)

And today, with your cutting-edge research programs and your new cyber initiatives, you're helping

WHAT THE GOVERNMENT AND POLITICIANS SAY

us navigate some of the most complicated cyber challenges that we face as a nation. And that's why we're here. I want to thank all of you who have joined us today -- members of Congress, representatives from the private sector, government, academia, privacy and consumer groups, and especially the students who are here. Just as we're all connected like never before, we have to work together like never before, both to seize opportunities but also meet the challenges of this Information Age.

And it's one of the great paradoxes of our time that the very technologies that empower us to do great good can also be used to undermine us and inflict great harm. The same information technologies that help make our military the most advanced in the world are targeted by hackers from China and Russia who go after our defense contractors and systems that are built for our troops. The same social media we use in government to advocate for democracy and human rights around the world can also be used by terrorists to spread hateful ideologies. So these cyber threats are a challenge to our national security.

Much of our critical infrastructure -- our financial systems, our power grid, health systems -- run on networks connected to the Internet, which is hugely empowering but also dangerous, and creates new points of vulnerability that we didn't have before. Foreign governments and criminals are probing these systems every single day. We only have to think of real-life examples -- an air traffic control system going down and disrupting flights, or blackouts that plunge cities into darkness -- to imagine what a set of systematic cyber attacks might do. So this is also a matter of public safety.

CRITICAL PERSPECTIVES ON CYBERWARFARE

As a nation, we do more business online than ever before -- trillions of dollars a year. And high-tech industries, like those across the Valley, support millions of American jobs. All this gives us an enormous competitive advantage in the global economy. And for that very reason, American companies are being targeted, their trade secrets stolen, intellectual property ripped off. The North Korean cyber attack on Sony Pictures destroyed data and disabled thousands of computers, and exposed the personal information of Sony employees. And these attacks are hurting American companies and costing American jobs. So this is also a threat to America's economic security.

As consumers, we do more online than ever before. We manage our bank accounts. We shop. We pay our bills. We handle our medical records. And as a country, one of our greatest resources are the young people who are here today --digitally fearless and unencumbered by convention, and uninterested in old debates. And they're remaking the world every day. But it also means that this problem of how we secure this digital world is only going to increase.

I want more Americans succeeding in our digital world. I want young people like you to unleash the next waves of innovation, and launch the next startups, and give Americans the tools to create new jobs and new businesses, and to expand connectivity in places that we currently can't imagine, to help open up new world and new experiences and empower individuals in ways that would seem unimaginable 10, 15, 20 years ago.

And that's why we're working to connect 99 percent of America's students to high-speed Internet -- because when it comes to educating our children, we can't afford any digital

WHAT THE GOVERNMENT AND POLITICIANS SAY

divides. It's why we're helping more communities get across to the next generation of broadband faster, with cheaper Internet, so that students and entrepreneurs and small businesses across America, not just in pockets of America, have the same opportunities to learn and compete as you do here in the Valley. It's why I've come out so strongly and publicly for net neutrality, for an open and free Internet -- (applause) -- because we have to preserve one of the greatest engines for creativity and innovation in human history.

So our connectivity brings extraordinary benefits to our daily lives, but it also brings risks. And when companies get hacked, Americans' personal information, including their financial information, gets stolen. Identity theft can ruin your credit rating and turn your life upside down. In recent breaches, more than 100 million Americans had their personal data compromised, including, in some cases, credit card information. We want our children to go online and explore the world, but we also want them to be safe and not have their privacy violated. So this is a direct threat to the economic security of American families, not just the economy overall, and to the well-being of our children, which means we've got to put in place mechanisms to protect them.

So shortly after I took office, before I had gray hair -- (laughter) -- I said that these cyber threats were one of the most serious economic national security challenges that we face as a nation, and I made confronting them a priority. And given the complexity of these threats, I believe we have to be guided by some basic principles. So let me share those with you today.

First, this has to be a shared mission. So much of our computer networks and critical infrastructure are in the private sector, which means government cannot do this alone. But the fact is that the private sector can't do it alone either, because it's government that often has the latest information on new threats. There's only one way to defend America from these cyber threats, and that is through government and industry working together, sharing appropriate information as true partners.

Second, we have to focus on our unique strengths. Government has many capabilities, but it's not appropriate or even possible for government to secure the computer networks of private businesses. Many of the companies who are here today are cutting-edge, but the private sector doesn't always have the capabilities needed during a cyber attack, the situational awareness, or the ability to warn other companies in real time, or the capacity to coordinate a response across companies and sectors. So we're going to have to be smart and efficient and focus on what each sector does best, and then do it together.

Third, we're going to have to constantly evolve. The first computer viruses hit personal computers in the early 1980s, and essentially, we've been in a cyber arms race ever since. We design new defenses, and then hackers and criminals design new ways to penetrate them. Whether it's phishing or botnets, spyware or malware, and now ransomware, these attacks are getting more and more sophisticated every day. So we've got to be just as fast and flexible and nimble in constantly evolving our defenses.

And fourth, and most importantly, in all our work we have to make sure we are protecting the privacy and civil liberty of the American people. And we grapple with these issues in government. We've pursued important reforms

WHAT THE GOVERNMENT AND POLITICIANS SAY

to make sure we are respecting peoples' privacy as well as ensuring our national security. And the private sector wrestles with this as well. When consumers share their personal information with companies, they deserve to know that it's going to be protected. When government and industry share information about cyber threats, we've got to do so in a way that safeguards your personal information. When people go online, we shouldn't have to forfeit the basic privacy we're entitled to as Americans.

In recent years, we've worked to put these principles into practice. And as part of our comprehensive strategy, we've boosted our defenses in government, we're sharing more information with the private sector to help those companies defend themselves, we're working with industry to use what we call a Cybersecurity Framework to prevent, respond to, and recover from attacks when they happen.

And, by the way, I recently went to the National Cybersecurity Communications Integration Center, which is part of the Department of Homeland Security, where representatives from government and the private sector monitor cyber threats 24/7. And so defending against cyber threats, just like terrorism or other threats, is one more reason that we are calling on Congress, not to engage in politics -- this is not a Republican or Democratic issue -- but work to make sure that our security is safeguarded and that we fully fund the Department of Homeland Security, because it has great responsibilities in this area.

So we're making progress, and I've recently announced new actions to keep up this momentum. We've called for a single national standard so Americans know within 30 days if your information has been stolen. This month, we'll be proposing legislation that we call a Consumer Privacy Bill of Rights to give Americans some baseline protections, like the right to decide what personal data companies collect from you, and the right to know how companies are using that information. We've proposed the Student Digital Privacy Act, which is modeled on the landmark law here in California -- because today's amazing educational technologies should be used to teach our students and not collect data for marketing to students.

And we've also taken new steps to strengthen our cybersecurity -- proposing new legislation to promote greater information sharing between government and the private sector, including liability protections for companies that share information about cyber threats. Today, I'm once again calling on Congress to come together and get this done.

And this week, we announced the creation of our new Cyber Threat Intelligence Integration Center. Just like we do with terrorist threats, we're going to have a single entity that's analyzing and integrating and quickly sharing intelligence about cyber threats across government so we can act on all those threats even faster.

And today, we're taking an additional step -- which is why there's a desk here. You were wondering, I'm sure. (Laughter.) I'm signing a new executive order to promote even more information sharing about cyber threats, both within the private sector and between government and the private sector. And it will encourage more companies and industries to set up organizations -- hubs -- so you can share information with each other. It will call for a common set of standards, including protections for

WHAT THE GOVERNMENT AND POLITICIANS SAY

privacy and civil liberties, so that government can share threat information with these hubs more easily. And it can help make it easier for companies to get the classified cybersecurity threat information that they need to protect their companies.

I want to acknowledge, by the way, that the companies who are represented here are stepping up as well. The Cyber Threat Alliance, which includes companies like Palo Alto Networks and Symantec, are going to work with us to share more information under this new executive order. You've got companies from Apple to Intel, from Bank of America to PG&E, who are going to use the Cybersecurity Framework to strengthen their own defenses. As part of our BuySecure Initiative, Visa and MasterCard and American Express and others are going to make their transactions more secure. Nationstar is joining companies that are giving their companies [customers] another weapon to battle identity theft, and that's free access to their credit scores.

And more companies are moving to new, stronger technologies to authenticate user identities, like biometrics -- because it's just too easy for hackers to figure out usernames and passwords, like "password." (Laughter.) Or "12345 -- (laughter) -- 7." (Laughter.) Those are some of my previous passwords. (Laughter.) I've changed them since then. (Applause.)

So this summit is an example of what we need more of -- all of us working together to do what none of us can achieve alone. And it is difficult. Some of the challenges I've described today have defied solutions for years. And I want to say very clearly that, as somebody who is a former constitutional law teacher, and somebody who deeply values his privacy and his family's privacy -- although I chose the wrong job for that -- (laughter) -- but will be a private citizen again, and cares deeply about this -- I have to tell you that grappling with how government protects the American people from adverse events while, at the same time, making sure that government itself is not abusing its capabilities is hard.

The cyber world is sort of the wild, wild West. And to some degree, we're asked to be the sheriff. When something like Sony happens, people want to know what can government do about this. If information is being shared by terrorists in the cyber world and an attack happens, people want to know are there ways of stopping that from happening. By necessity, that means government has its own significant capabilities in the cyber world. But then people, rightly, ask, well, what safeguards do we have against government intruding on our own privacy? And it's hard, and it constantly evolves because the technology so often outstrips whatever rules and structures and standards have been put in place, which means that government has to be constantly self-critical and we have to be able to have an open debate about it.

But we're all here today because we know that we're going to have to break through some of these barriers that are holding us back if we are going to continue to thrive in this remarkable new world. We all know what we need to do. We have to build stronger defenses and disrupt more attacks. We have to make cyberspace safer. We have to improve cooperation across the board. And, by the way, this is not just here in America, but internationally -- which also, by the way, makes things complicated because a lot of countries

WHAT THE GOVERNMENT AND POLITICIANS SAY

don't necessarily share our investment -- or our commitment to openness, and we have to try to navigate that.

But this should not be an ideological issue. And that's one thing I want to emphasize: This is not a Democratic issue, or a Republican issue. This is not a liberal or conservative issue. Everybody is online, and everybody is vulnerable. The business leaders here want their privacy and their children protected, just like the consumer and privacy advocates here want America to keep leading the world in technology and be safe from attacks. So I'm hopeful that through this forum and the work that we do subsequently, that we're able to generate ideas and best practices, and that the work of this summit can help guide our planning and execution for years to come.

After all, we are just getting started. Think about it. Tim Berners-Lee, from his lab in Switzerland, invented the World Wide Web in 1989, which was only 26 years ago. The great epochs in human history -- the Bronze Age, Iron Age, Agricultural Revolution, Industrial Revolution -- they spanned centuries. We're only 26 years into this Internet Age. We've only scratched the surface. And as I guess they say at Google, "The future is awesome." (Laughter.) We haven't even begun to imagine the discoveries and innovations that are going to be unleashed in the decades to come. But we know how we'll get there.

Reflecting on his work in the 1960s on ARPANET, the precursor of the Internet, the late Paul Baran said this: "The process of technological developments is like building a cathedral. Over the course of several hundred years, new people come along and each lays down a block on top of the old foundations, each saying, 'I built the cathedral.' And then comes along an historian who

CRITICAL PERSPECTIVES ON CYBERWARFARE

asks, 'Well, who built the cathedral?'" And Baran said, "If you're not careful, you can con yourself into believing that you did the most important part. But the reality is that each contribution has to follow on to previous work. Everything is tied to everything else."

Everything is tied to everything else. The innovations that first appeared on this campus all those decades ago -- that first mouse, that first message -- helped lay a foundation. And in the decades since, on campuses like this, in companies like those that are represented here, new people have come along, each laying down a block, one on top of the other. And when future historians ask who built this Information Age, it won't be any one of us who did the most important part alone. The answer will be, "We all did, as Americans."

And I'm absolutely confident that if we keep at this, if we keep working together in a spirit of collaboration, like all those innovators before us, our work will endure, like a great cathedral, for centuries to come. And that cathedral will not just be about technology, it will be about the values that we've embedded in the architecture of this system. It will be about privacy, and it will be about community. And it will be about connection. What a magnificent cathedral that all of you have helped to build. We want to be a part of that, and we look forward to working with you in the future.

Thank you for your partnership. With that, I'm going to sign this executive order. Thank you. (Applause.)

1. President Barack Obama discusses how difficult it is for people to know whether they want the government

more or less involved in cybersecurity. He mentions that when something like the Sony hack occurs, people want more government help, but that people are also afraid of what it means if the government has that much power online. Do you think it's possible for the government to strike the right balance between having the power to help people without making people worry they'll abuse it?

2. What are some steps you think the government should take to help protect citizens from hacks by foreign actors?

"REMARKS BY HOMELAND SECURITY ADVISOR THOMAS P. BOSSERT AT CYBER WEEK 2017," BY THOMAS P. BOSSERT, FROM THE WHITE HOUSE, JUNE 26, 2017

Thank you for that kind introduction. It is an honor to be here today on behalf of President Trump and the American people.

Thank you, Prime Minister Netanyahu, Dr. Matania, and the wonderful conference hosts for inviting me. I'm humbled to speak at this important event to such a distinguished group.

This incredible event includes cyber professionals from more than 50 countries. Those of you that are here for Cyber Week are among the world's most accomplished experts in this field. Thank you for what you do, and for what you will continue to do when this week together ends and you return to your jobs around the globe.

Prime Minister Netanyahu, I know our relations are strong; and judging from this audience, it's clear you can draw more U.S. talent into one room than I can.

I am here to talk about Cybersecurity. I am also here because President Trump understands the U.S. cannot lessen our engagement in this region of the world, lessen our support for Israel, or create a power vacuum for Iran, ISIS, Hezbollah, and Hamas to fill. Doing so would make the world a more dangerous place.

I am pleased to be here with a Prime Minister who voiced his clear-eyed objection to appeasing Iran and enabling its nuclear aspirations. He did so at great professional risk and took political criticism for stating an unpopular truth. He was right. He was courageous. The American people agreed with him. And now, he has a partner in President Trump and the Israeli people have a stronger, deeper relationship with the United States because of it.

PM Netanyahu will continue to defend the State of Israel.

President Trump's May visit demonstrated our continued commitment to Israel. We remain particularly close on security issues. America's security partnership with Israel is stronger than ever. The Iron Dome missile defense program continues to keep the Israeli people safe from short-range rockets launched by Hezbollah and Hamas. The David's Sling and Arrow weapons systems guard against long-range missiles. We hope that someday soon we live in a world where children will never need to rush towards shelter, as sirens ring out.

There is incredible technology in the Iron Dome system. It is that kind of ingenuity that we need to tap as the fight moves from missiles in the air to malware through the Internet.

President Trump said something else on his recent trip here – his first international trip – he said that Israel is a testament to the unbreakable spirit of the Jewish people. From all parts of this great country, one message resounds: and that is the message of hope. That message of hope extends to the Palestinian people as well.

He brought a message that we must build a coalition of partners who aim to stamp out violent extremism.

Cyberspace has emerged as a major arena of conflict between liberal and illiberal forces across the globe, making the interconnected world of cyberspace one of the biggest strategic challenges since 9/11.

Israel is a market oriented, knowledge-based economy with a strong technology sector. You have the highest research and development spending per GDP in the world. And, one of the most talented tech workforces in the world – and a system for developing that talent that we can all learn from.

So, it's not surprising that the leadership of Israel would support events such as this to bring together the best and brightest minds to address today's challenges in the cyber environment. While physical borders can be extremely important, cyberspace knows no boundaries.

Nations increasingly have the ability to steal sensitive information, alter data, or even destroy systems. And the trend is heading in the wrong direction.

Destructive attacks are being executed by belligerent nations. North Korea attacked Sony, and Iran attacked Sands Casino and Saudi Aramco. Neither of these countries have near the sophistication and resources of China and Russia. And, we cannot forget the challenges facing our small- and mid-sized businesses – the backbones of our economies – who are facing threats from ransomware to the theft of their intellectual property by foreign intelligence services.

Cyber threats continue to grow. The complexity of the challenge continues to allude us. The question is: What is standing in our adversary's way?

Part of the answer includes firewalls, anti-virus, good network hygiene, etc. Better and faster information sharing is also suppressing malicious activity. These are all things we are promoting in the United States and improving in the Trump Administration.

Yet, this would have been the same answer 15 years ago.

And, while these are good and necessary things, the adversary doesn't encounter them until he's compromised his target's network.

Today – 15 years later – we're introducing terms like artificial intelligence and machine learning. We have ways of sharing information and ways to orchestrate defenses in our networks faster than we could have ever before. Again – all good and necessary. Better and faster, but not different. And, always after the adversary is in his target's system.

I would like this audience, this week, to advance the conversation. The Israelis and others have adopted operational constructs between the public and private sectors that focus on the adversary; what the adversary is doing in

WHAT THE GOVERNMENT AND POLITICIANS SAY

the internet; and how to thwart, impede, or otherwise inflict a defensive cost on the adversary, or—when necessary—deter bad behavior with punitive measures.

We must recognize that while we have small differences, free and market-based nations must engage with the private sector in an OPERATIONAL way to identify our cyber adversaries and increase our defenses considerably. And, we can do it in a way that preserves our privacy and security, while safeguarding our intelligence sources and methods.

Cybersecurity is about risk management. Networked technology will never be completely secure, and we need to prioritize our work.

We need to mitigate and manage risk; this includes identifying key data and the functions that must be protected, and then deliberately planning for their protection. We must centralize policies in government and industry, and decentralize their execution. And, we need standards and metrics to hold managers accountable. We must implement fundamental cybersecurity practices; to include regular patching, multifactor authentication, encrypting data, at rest and in motion, and white-listing applications.

We must also secure our nations; this includes defending our critical infrastructure and focusing on the energy sector, communications, financial services, and transportation; the lifeline sectors. There is a clear role for government in this work. This priority, while it has been subject to countless discussions, has not seen the progress it deserves.

Across the globe there are countries that do this with greater success than others. Israel is an example. We cannot achieve the security we need without partnerships. Partnerships with industry, partnerships with the owners and operators of infrastructure, and partnerships with likeminded countries.

Increased defense is critical. As is deterrence. We must get serious about a deterrence strategy. The stakes are too high and the risks are too grave not to. This requires a foundational understanding of what constitutes responsible behavior, and what is unacceptable.

Progress has been made in building consensus around responsible state behavior and the Trump Administration will work to expand that consensus. We must move from talking about norms to implementing them. But we must also hold those who violate these norms accountable.

This may not be achievable through a UN effort. Just last week, we saw the limits of the UN Group of Governmental Experts, which had achieved some good results in the past, but came up short. They were unable to even reach consensus on their final report.

It's time to consider other approaches. We will also work with smaller groups of likeminded partners to call out bad behavior and impose costs on our adversaries. We will also pursue bilateral agreements when needed.

Deterrence may require limiting bad actors' access to our markets and other benefits the Internet brings. These are the questions we must ask. There should be incentives for cooperation and consequences for disruption. I think that needs to be stated out loud.

While not abandoning our multilateral efforts, the United States will move forward internationally in meaningful bilateral efforts, such as the one we enjoy with Great Britain and now Israel, while continuing to build a likeminded coalition of partners who can act together.

WHAT THE GOVERNMENT AND POLITICIANS SAY

The cyber strategies of the future must draw upon the clear experience of history. The only way to provide a safer and more secure future in a digitally connected world is to embrace the principles of individual property; the rule of law; and an unwavering commitment to free markets. And, to exclude those who do not.

We share these values with many nations around the world, including Israel. We know nations that are economically and politically free will always be stronger than nations that are not. There has been no better engine for capitalism and growth than the internet. Consider the wealth and development that cyberspace has enabled. The internet reflecting our values is where we will find partners sharing those values.

Nations that share these values also know the role of government is to apply rules to protect them. The free market succeeds because of basic rules observed between individuals and also rules designed by government to protect contracts and promises and transfers of goods and services. When this is threatened within a nation or internationally, it is appropriate for the government to respond.

The system works in part because those who violate the rules suffer consequences, and those who act well do well. So, if individuals or nations choose to manipulate cyberspace for financial gain or geopolitical advantage, we must act to protect our shared values.

The Internet is a great example of the free market at work. No capitalist is surprised that the Internet was invented in a free society. The Internet was invented in America, by Americans—and one Brit—with government help. Yet, it was private industry that turned the Internet into one of the world's greatest tools. Despite this success,

73

the Internet is vulnerable to fragmenting and we need to push back.

The next step must be gaining international cooperation to impose consequences on those that act contrary to this growing consensus.

To accomplish this, likeminded states should work to develop options for imposing consequences within a coalition structure, if possible. Until then, the United States must seek partners bilaterally.

And so, it is with great pleasure I can announce TODAY the commencement of a U.S.-Israel bilateral cyber working group, led by Mr. Rob Joyce, the White House Cybersecurity Coordinator and Dr. Matania (weren't they great?), along with the Department of State and representatives from the Departments of Commerce, Defense, and Homeland Security, and the FBI.

The U.S. delegation will meet with senior leaders from Israel's National Cyber Bureau, Defense Force, Shin Bet and Ministries of Foreign Affairs, Justice, and Defense. The meetings this week will focus on a range of cyber issues — critical infrastructure, advanced R&D, international cooperation, and workforce development, among others. These high-level meetings represent the first step in strengthening bilateral ties on cyber issues following President Trump's visit to Israel, and they make good on the promise he made to Prime Minister Netanyahu at their meeting on February 15.

The bi-lateral working group of experts from across agencies will work with an eye towards developing a different operational construct: focused on finding and stopping cyber adversaries before they are in your networks; before they reach critical infrastructure, and

WHAT THE GOVERNMENT AND POLITICIANS SAY

identifying ways to hold bad actors accountable—a different conversation indeed.

We believe that the agility Israel has in developing solutions will result in innovative cyber defenses we can test here and then take back to America.

Over the course of this week, the assembled group here today will develop ideas that will advance cybersecurity and produce recommendations from industry on best practices, implementation, and execution concepts. Perfect security may not be achievable, but we have within our reach a safer, more secure Internet. I look forward to the progress we'll make together in this endeavor.

I thank you very much for your time and I look forward to the future.

1. In his speech, Bossert says that it doesn't take sophisticated skills or technology to launch a successful cyberattack, and he points to attacks by North Korea and Israel as examples. If Bossert is right, what do you think that means for the future of cyberwarfare?

2. Bossert says that experts in government and in corporate technology fields need to work together to combat cyberattacks. With what you've learned, how do you think these two sides can work together to create better cybersecurity?

"PRESIDENTIAL EXECUTIVE ORDER ON STRENGTHENING THE CYBERSECURITY OF FEDERAL NETWORKS AND CRITICAL INFRASTRUCTURE," BY PRESIDENT DONALD TRUMP, FROM THE WHITE HOUSE, MAY 11, 2017

By the authority vested in me as President by the Constitution and the laws of the United States of America, and to protect American innovation and values, it is hereby ordered as follows:

Section 1. Cybersecurity of Federal Networks.

(a) Policy. The executive branch operates its information technology (IT) on behalf of the American people. Its IT and data should be secured responsibly using all United States Government capabilities. The President will hold heads of executive departments and agencies (agency heads) accountable for managing cybersecurity risk to their enterprises. In addition, because risk management decisions made by agency heads can affect the risk to the executive branch as a whole, and to national security, it is also the policy of the United States to manage cybersecurity risk as an executive branch enterprise.

(b) Findings.

(i) Cybersecurity risk management comprises the full range of activities undertaken to protect IT and

WHAT THE GOVERNMENT AND POLITICIANS SAY

data from unauthorized access and other cyber threats, to maintain awareness of cyber threats, to detect anomalies and incidents adversely affecting IT and data, and to mitigate the impact of, respond to, and recover from incidents. Information sharing facilitates and supports all of these activities.

(ii) The executive branch has for too long accepted antiquated and difficult-to-defend IT.

(iii) Effective risk management involves more than just protecting IT and data currently in place. It also requires planning so that maintenance, improvements, and modernization occur in a coordinated way and with appropriate regularity.

(iv) Known but unmitigated vulnerabilities are among the highest cybersecurity risks faced by executive departments and agencies (agencies). Known vulnerabilities include using operating systems or hardware beyond the vendor's support lifecycle, declining to implement a vendor's security patch, or failing to execute security-specific configuration guidance.

(v) Effective risk management requires agency heads to lead integrated teams of senior executives with expertise in IT, security, budgeting, acquisition, law, privacy, and human resources.

(c) Risk Management.

(i) Agency heads will be held accountable by the President for implementing risk management measures commensurate with the risk and magnitude of the harm that would result from unauthorized access, use, disclosure, disruption, modification, or destruction of IT and data. They will also be held accountable by the President for ensuring that cybersecurity risk management processes are aligned with strategic, operational, and budgetary planning processes, in accordance with chapter 35, subchapter II of title 44, United States Code.

(ii) Effective immediately, each agency head shall use The Framework for Improving Critical Infrastructure Cybersecurity (the Framework) developed by the National Institute of Standards and Technology, or any successor document, to manage the agency's cybersecurity risk. Each agency head shall provide a risk management report to the Secretary of Homeland Security and the Director of the Office of Management and Budget (OMB) within 90 days of the date of this order. The risk management report shall:

(A) document the risk mitigation and acceptance choices made by each agency head as of the date of this order, including:

(1) the strategic, operational, and budgetary considerations that informed those choices; and

(2) any accepted risk, including from unmitigated vulnerabilities; and

(B) describe the agency's action plan to implement the Framework.

WHAT THE GOVERNMENT AND POLITICIANS SAY

(iii) The Secretary of Homeland Security and the Director of OMB, consistent with chapter 35, subchapter II of title 44, United States Code, shall jointly assess each agency's risk management report to determine whether the risk mitigation and acceptance choices set forth in the reports are appropriate and sufficient to manage the cybersecurity risk to the executive branch enterprise in the aggregate (the determination).

(iv) The Director of OMB, in coordination with the Secretary of Homeland Security, with appropriate support from the Secretary of Commerce and the Administrator of General Services, and within 60 days of receipt of the agency risk management reports outlined in subsection (c)(ii) of this section, shall submit to the President, through the Assistant to the President for Homeland Security and Counterterrorism, the following:

(A) the determination; and

(B) a plan to:

(1) adequately protect the executive branch enterprise, should the determination identify insufficiencies;

(2) address immediate unmet budgetary needs necessary to manage risk to the executive branch enterprise;

(3) establish a regular process for reassessing and, if appropriate, reissuing the determination, and addressing future, recurring unmet budgetary needs necessary to manage risk to the executive branch enterprise;

(4) clarify, reconcile, and reissue, as necessary and to the extent permitted by law, all policies, standards, and guidelines issued by any agency in furtherance of chapter 35, subchapter II of title 44, United States Code, and, as necessary and to the extent permitted by law, issue policies, standards, and guidelines in furtherance of this order; and

(5) align these policies, standards, and guidelines with the Framework.

(v) The agency risk management reports described in subsection (c)(ii) of this section and the determination and plan described in subsections (c)(iii) and (iv) of this section may be classified in full or in part, as appropriate.

(vi) Effective immediately, it is the policy of the executive branch to build and maintain a modern, secure, and more resilient executive branch IT architecture.

(A) Agency heads shall show preference in their procurement for shared IT services, to the extent permitted by law, including email, cloud, and cybersecurity services.

(B) The Director of the American Technology Council shall coordinate a report to the President from the Secretary of Homeland Security, the Director of OMB, and the Administrator of General Services, in consultation with the Secretary of Commerce, as appropriate, regarding modernization of Federal IT. The report shall:

WHAT THE GOVERNMENT AND POLITICIANS SAY

(1) be completed within 90 days of the date of this order; and

(2) describe the legal, policy, and budgetary considerations relevant to -- as well as the technical feasibility and cost effectiveness, including timelines and milestones, of -- transitioning all agencies, or a subset of agencies, to:

(aa) one or more consolidated network architectures; and

(bb) shared IT services, including email, cloud, and cybersecurity services.

(C) The report described in subsection (c)(vi)(B) of this section shall assess the effects of transitioning all agencies, or a subset of agencies, to shared IT services with respect to cybersecurity, including by making recommendations to ensure consistency with section 227 of the Homeland Security Act (6 U.S.C. 148) and compliance with policies and practices issued in accordance with section 3553 of title 44, United States Code. All agency heads shall supply such information concerning their current IT architectures and plans as is necessary to complete this report on time.

(vii) For any National Security System, as defined in section 3552(b)(6) of title 44, United States Code, the Secretary of Defense and the Director of National Intelligence, rather than the Secretary of Homeland Security and the Director of OMB, shall implement this order to the maximum extent feasible and appropriate. The Secretary of Defense and the Director of National Intelligence shall provide a report to the Assistant to the President for National Security Affairs and the Assistant to the President for Homeland Security and Counterterrorism describing their implementation of subsection (c) of this section within 150 days of the date of this order. The report described in this subsection shall include a justification for any deviation from the requirements of subsection (c), and may be classified in full or in part, as appropriate.

Sec. 2. Cybersecurity of Critical Infrastructure.

(a) Policy. It is the policy of the executive branch to use its authorities and capabilities to support the cybersecurity risk management efforts of the owners and operators of the Nation's critical infrastructure (as defined in section 5195c(e) of title 42, United States Code) (critical infrastructure entities), as appropriate.

(b) Support to Critical Infrastructure at Greatest Risk. The Secretary of Homeland Security, in coordination with the Secretary of Defense, the Attorney General, the Director of National Intelligence, the Director of the Federal Bureau of Investigation, the heads of appropriate sector-specific agencies, as defined in Presidential Policy Directive 21 of February 12, 2013 (Critical Infrastructure Security and Resilience) (sector-specific agencies), and all other appropriate agency heads, as identified by the Secretary of Homeland Security, shall:

(i) identify authorities and capabilities that agencies could employ to support the cybersecurity efforts of critical infrastructure entities identified pursuant to section 9 of Executive Order 13636 of February 12, 2013 (Improving Critical Infrastructure Cybersecurity), to be at greatest risk of attacks that could reasonably result in catastrophic regional or national effects on public health or safety, economic security, or national security (section 9 entities);

(ii) engage section 9 entities and solicit input as appropriate to evaluate whether and how the authorities and capabilities identified pursuant to subsection (b)(i) of this section might be employed to support cybersecurity risk management efforts and any obstacles to doing so;

(iii) provide a report to the President, which may be classified in full or in part, as appropriate, through the Assistant to the President for Homeland Security and Counterterrorism, within 180 days of the date of this order, that includes the following:

(A) the authorities and capabilities identified pursuant to subsection (b)(i) of this section;

(B) the results of the engagement and determination required pursuant to subsection (b)(ii) of this section; and

(C) findings and recommendations for better supporting the cybersecurity risk management efforts of section 9 entities; and

(iv) provide an updated report to the President on an annual basis thereafter.

(c) Supporting Transparency in the Marketplace. The Secretary of Homeland Security, in coordination with the Secretary of Commerce, shall provide a report to the President, through the Assistant to the President for Homeland Security and Counterterrorism, that examines the sufficiency of existing Federal policies and practices to promote appropriate market transparency of cybersecurity risk management practices by critical infrastructure entities, with a focus on publicly traded critical infrastructure entities, within 90 days of the date of this order.

(d) Resilience Against Botnets and Other Automated, Distributed Threats. The Secretary of Commerce and the Secretary of Homeland Security shall jointly lead an open and transparent process to identify and promote action by appropriate stakeholders to improve the resilience of the internet and communications ecosystem and to encourage collaboration with the goal of dramatically reducing threats perpetrated by automated and distributed attacks (e.g., botnets). The Secretary of Commerce and the Secretary of Homeland Security shall consult with the Secretary of Defense, the Attorney General, the Director of the Federal Bureau of Investigation, the heads of sector-specific agencies, the Chairs of the Federal Communications Commission and Federal Trade Commission, other interested agency heads, and appropriate stakeholders in carrying out this subsection. Within 240 days of the date of this order, the Secretary of Commerce and the Secretary of Homeland Security shall make publicly available a preliminary report on this effort. Within 1 year of the date of this order, the Secretaries shall submit a final version of this report to the President.

(e) Assessment of Electricity Disruption Incident Response Capabilities. The Secretary of Energy and the Secretary of Homeland Security, in consultation with the Director of National Intelligence, with State, local, tribal, and territorial governments, and with others as appropriate, shall jointly assess:

(i) the potential scope and duration of a prolonged power outage associated with a significant cyber incident, as defined in Presidential Policy Directive 41 of July 26, 2016 (United States Cyber Incident Coordination), against the United States electric subsector;

(ii) the readiness of the United States to manage the consequences of such an incident; and

(iii) any gaps or shortcomings in assets or capabilities required to mitigate the consequences of such an incident.

The assessment shall be provided to the President, through the Assistant to the President for Homeland Security and Counterterrorism, within 90 days of the date of this order, and may be classified in full or in part, as appropriate.

(f) Department of Defense Warfighting Capabilities and Industrial Base. Within 90 days of the date of this order, the Secretary of Defense, the Secretary of Homeland Security, and the Director of the Federal Bureau of Investigation, in coordination with the Director of National Intelligence, shall provide a report to the President, through the Assistant to the President for National Security Affairs and the Assistant to the President for Homeland Security and Counterterrorism, on cybersecurity risks facing the defense industrial base, including its supply chain, and United States military platforms, systems, networks, and capabilities, and recommendations for mitigating these risks. The report may be classified in full or in part, as appropriate.

Sec. 3. Cybersecurity for the Nation.

(a) Policy. To ensure that the internet remains valuable for future generations, it is the policy of the executive branch to promote an open, interoperable, reliable, and secure internet that fosters efficiency, innovation, communication, and economic prosperity, while respecting privacy and guarding against disruption, fraud, and theft. Further, the United States seeks to support the growth and sustainment of a workforce that is skilled in cybersecurity and related fields as the foundation for achieving our objectives in cyberspace.

(b) Deterrence and Protection. Within 90 days of the date of this order, the Secretary of State, the Secretary of the Treasury, the Secretary of Defense, the Attorney General, the Secretary of Commerce, the Secretary of Homeland Security, and the United States Trade Representative, in coordination with the Director of

National Intelligence, shall jointly submit a report to the President, through the Assistant to the President for National Security Affairs and the Assistant to the President for Homeland Security and Counterterrorism, on the Nation's strategic options for deterring adversaries and better protecting the American people from cyber threats.

(c) International Cooperation. As a highly connected nation, the United States is especially dependent on a globally secure and resilient internet and must work with allies and other partners toward maintaining the policy set forth in this section. Within 45 days of the date of this order, the Secretary of State, the Secretary of the Treasury, the Secretary of Defense, the Secretary of Commerce, and the Secretary of Homeland Security, in coordination with the Attorney General and the Director of the Federal Bureau of Investigation, shall submit reports to the President on their international cybersecurity priorities, including those concerning investigation, attribution, cyber threat information sharing, response, capacity building, and cooperation. Within 90 days of the submission of the reports, and in coordination with the agency heads listed in this subsection, and any other agency heads as appropriate, the Secretary of State shall provide a report to the President, through the Assistant to the President for Homeland Security and Counterterrorism, documenting an engagement strategy for international cooperation in cybersecurity.

(d) Workforce Development. In order to ensure that the United States maintains a long-term cybersecurity advantage:

(i) The Secretary of Commerce and the Secretary of Homeland Security, in consultation with the Secretary of Defense, the Secretary of Labor, the Secretary of Education, the Director of the Office of Personnel Management, and other agencies identified jointly by the Secretary of Commerce and the Secretary of Homeland Security, shall:

(A) jointly assess the scope and sufficiency of efforts to educate and train the American cybersecurity workforce of the future, including cybersecurity-related education curricula, training, and apprenticeship programs, from primary through higher education; and

(B) within 120 days of the date of this order, provide a report to the President, through the Assistant to the President for Homeland Security and Counterterrorism, with findings and recommendations regarding how to support the growth and sustainment of the Nation's cybersecurity workforce in both the public and private sectors.

(ii) The Director of National Intelligence, in consultation with the heads of other agencies identified by the Director of National Intelligence, shall:

(A) review the workforce development efforts of potential foreign cyber peers in order to help identify foreign workforce development practices likely to affect long-term United States cybersecurity competitiveness; and

(B) within 60 days of the date of this order, provide a report to the President through the Assistant to the President for Homeland Security and Counterterrorism on the findings of the review carried out pursuant to subsection (d)(ii)(A) of this section.

(iii) The Secretary of Defense, in coordination with the Secretary of Commerce, the Secretary of Homeland Security, and the Director of National Intelligence, shall:

(A) assess the scope and sufficiency of United States efforts to ensure that the United States maintains or increases its advantage in national-security-related cyber capabilities; and

(B) within 150 days of the date of this order, provide a report to the President, through the Assistant to the President for Homeland Security and Counterterrorism, with findings and recommendations on the assessment carried out pursuant to subsection (d)(iii)(A) of this section.

(iv) The reports described in this subsection may be classified in full or in part, as appropriate.

Sec. 4. Definitions. For the purposes of this order:

(a) The term "appropriate stakeholders" means any non-executive-branch person or entity that elects to participate in an open and transparent process established by the Secretary of Commerce and the Secretary of Homeland Security under section 2(d) of this order.

(b) The term "information technology" (IT) has the meaning given to that term in section 11101(6) of title 40,

United States Code, and further includes hardware and software systems of agencies that monitor and control physical equipment and processes.

(c) The term "IT architecture" refers to the integration and implementation of IT within an agency.

(d) The term "network architecture" refers to the elements of IT architecture that enable or facilitate communications between two or more IT assets.

Sec. 5. General Provisions. (a) Nothing in this order shall be construed to impair or otherwise affect:

(i) the authority granted by law to an executive department or agency, or the head thereof; or

(ii) the functions of the Director of OMB relating to budgetary, administrative, or legislative proposals.

(b) This order shall be implemented consistent with applicable law and subject to the availability of appropriations.

(c) All actions taken pursuant to this order shall be consistent with requirements and authorities to protect intelligence and law enforcement sources and methods. Nothing in this order shall be construed to supersede measures established under authority of law to protect the security and integrity of specific activities and associations that are in direct support of intelligence or law enforcement operations.

WHAT THE GOVERNMENT AND POLITICIANS SAY

(d) This order is not intended to, and does not, create any right or benefit, substantive or procedural, enforceable at law or in equity by any party against the United States, its departments, agencies, or entities, its officers, employees, or agents, or any other person.

1. In President Trump's executive order, he talks about the need for better education for future cybersecurity professionals. In addition to programming and hacking skills, what are some noncyber skills you think should be included in this curriculum to better train cybersecurity students for their work?

2. The order says that part of the job of cybersecurity professionals is to be aware of possible future threats. Given what you've learned so far, do you think this is possible? How can people be better aware of potential threats against their own digital worlds?

"REMARKS BY THE PRESIDENT ON SECURING OUR NATION'S CYBER INFRASTRUCTURE," BY BARACK OBAMA, FROM THE WHITE HOUSE ARCHIVES, MAY 29, 2009

Everybody, please be seated. We meet today at a transformational moment -- a moment in history when our interconnected world presents us, at once, with great promise but also great peril.

Now, over the past four months my administration has taken decisive steps to seize the promise and confront these perils. We're working to recover from a global recession while laying a new foundation for lasting prosperity. We're strengthening our armed forces as they fight two wars, at the same time we're renewing American leadership to confront unconventional challenges, from nuclear proliferation to terrorism, from climate change to pandemic disease. And we're bringing to government -- and to this White House -- unprecedented transparency and accountability and new ways for Americans to participate in their democracy.

But none of this progress would be possible, and none of these 21st century challenges can be fully met, without America's digital infrastructure -- the backbone that underpins a prosperous economy and a strong military and an open and efficient government. Without that foundation we can't get the job done.

It's long been said that the revolutions in communications and information technology have given birth to a virtual world. But make no mistake: This world -- cyberspace -- is a world that we depend on every single day. It's

WHAT THE GOVERNMENT AND POLITICIANS SAY

our hardware and our software, our desktops and laptops and cell phones and Blackberries that have become woven into every aspect of our lives.

It's the broadband networks beneath us and the wireless signals around us, the local networks in our schools and hospitals and businesses, and the massive grids that power our nation. It's the classified military and intelligence networks that keep us safe, and the World Wide Web that has made us more interconnected than at any time in human history.

So cyberspace is real. And so are the risks that come with it.

It's the great irony of our Information Age -- the very technologies that empower us to create and to build also empower those who would disrupt and destroy. And this paradox -- seen and unseen -- is something that we experience every day.

It's about the privacy and the economic security of American families. We rely on the Internet to pay our bills, to bank, to shop, to file our taxes. But we've had to learn a whole new vocabulary just to stay ahead of the cyber criminals who would do us harm -- spyware and malware and spoofing and phishing and botnets. Millions of Americans have been victimized, their privacy violated, their identities stolen, their lives upended, and their wallets emptied. According to one survey, in the past two years alone cyber crime has cost Americans more than $8 billion.

I know how it feels to have privacy violated because it has happened to me and the people around me. It's no secret that my presidential campaign harnessed the

CRITICAL PERSPECTIVES ON CYBERWARFARE

Internet and technology to transform our politics. What isn't widely known is that during the general election hackers managed to penetrate our computer systems. To all of you who donated to our campaign, I want you to all rest assured, our fundraising website was untouched. (Laughter.) So your confidential personal and financial information was protected.

But between August and October, hackers gained access to emails and a range of campaign files, from policy position papers to travel plans. And we worked closely with the CIA -- with the FBI and the Secret Service and hired security consultants to restore the security of our systems. It was a powerful reminder: In this Information Age, one of your greatest strengths -- in our case, our ability to communicate to a wide range of supporters through the Internet -- could also be one of your greatest vulnerabilities.

This is a matter, as well, of America's economic competitiveness. The small businesswoman in St. Louis, the bond trader in the New York Stock Exchange, the workers at a global shipping company in Memphis, the young entrepreneur in Silicon Valley -- they all need the networks to make the next payroll, the next trade, the next delivery, the next great breakthrough. E-commerce alone last year accounted for some $132 billion in retail sales.

But every day we see waves of cyber thieves trolling for sensitive information -- the disgruntled employee on the inside, the lone hacker a thousand miles away, organized crime, the industrial spy and, increasingly, foreign intelligence services. In one brazen act last year, thieves used stolen credit card

WHAT THE GOVERNMENT AND POLITICIANS SAY

information to steal millions of dollars from 130 ATM machines in 49 cities around the world -- and they did it in just 30 minutes. A single employee of an American company was convicted of stealing intellectual property reportedly worth $400 million. It's been estimated that last year alone cyber criminals stole intellectual property from businesses worldwide worth up to $1 trillion.

In short, America's economic prosperity in the 21st century will depend on cybersecurity.

And this is also a matter of public safety and national security. We count on computer networks to deliver our oil and gas, our power and our water. We rely on them for public transportation and air traffic control. Yet we know that cyber intruders have probed our electrical grid and that in other countries cyber attacks have plunged entire cities into darkness.

Our technological advantage is a key to America's military dominance. But our defense and military networks are under constant attack. Al Qaeda and other terrorist groups have spoken of their desire to unleash a cyber attack on our country -- attacks that are harder to detect and harder to defend against. Indeed, in today's world, acts of terror could come not only from a few extremists in suicide vests but from a few key strokes on the computer -- a weapon of mass disruption.

In one of the most serious cyber incidents to date against our military networks, several thousand computers were infected last year by malicious software -- malware. And while no sensitive information was compromised, our troops and defense personnel had to give up those external memory devices -- thumb drives -- changing the way they used their computers every day.

And last year we had a glimpse of the future face of war. As Russian tanks rolled into Georgia, cyber attacks crippled Georgian government websites. The terrorists that sowed so much death and destruction in Mumbai relied not only on guns and grenades but also on GPS and phones using voice-over-the-Internet.

For all these reasons, it's now clear this cyber threat is one of the most serious economic and national security challenges we face as a nation.

It's also clear that we're not as prepared as we should be, as a government or as a country. In recent years, some progress has been made at the federal level. But just as we failed in the past to invest in our physical infrastructure -- our roads, our bridges and rails -- we've failed to invest in the security of our digital infrastructure.

No single official oversees cybersecurity policy across the federal government, and no single agency has the responsibility or authority to match the scope and scale of the challenge. Indeed, when it comes to cybersecurity, federal agencies have overlapping missions and don't coordinate and communicate nearly as well as they should -- with each other or with the private sector. We saw this in the disorganized response to Conficker, the Internet "worm" that in recent months has infected millions of computers around the world.

This status quo is no longer acceptable -- not when there's so much at stake. We can and we must do better.

And that's why shortly after taking office I directed my National Security Council and Homeland Security Council to conduct a top-to-bottom review of the federal government's efforts to defend our information and communications infrastructure and to recommend the best way to

WHAT THE GOVERNMENT AND POLITICIANS SAY

ensure that these networks are able to secure our networks as well as our prosperity.

Our review was open and transparent. I want to acknowledge, Melissa Hathaway, who is here, who is the Acting Senior Director for Cyberspace on our National Security Council, who led the review team, as well as the Center for Strategic and International Studies bipartisan Commission on Cybersecurity, and all who were part of our 60-day review team. They listened to a wide variety of groups, many of which are represented here today and I want to thank for their input: industry and academia, civil liberties and private -- privacy advocates. We listened to every level and branch of government -- from local to state to federal, civilian, military, homeland as well as intelligence, Congress and international partners, as well. I consulted with my national security teams, my homeland security teams, and my economic advisors.

Today I'm releasing a report on our review, and can announce that my administration will pursue a new comprehensive approach to securing America's digital infrastructure.

This new approach starts at the top, with this commitment from me: From now on, our digital infrastructure -- the networks and computers we depend on every day -- will be treated as they should be: as a strategic national asset. Protecting this infrastructure will be a national security priority. We will ensure that these networks are secure, trustworthy and resilient. We will deter, prevent, detect, and defend against attacks and recover quickly from any disruptions or damage.

To give these efforts the high-level focus and attention they deserve -- and as part of the new, single National

Security Staff announced this week -- I'm creating a new office here at the White House that will be led by the Cybersecurity Coordinator. Because of the critical importance of this work, I will personally select this official. I'll depend on this official in all matters relating to cybersecurity, and this official will have my full support and regular access to me as we confront these challenges.

Today, I want to focus on the important responsibilities this office will fulfill: orchestrating and integrating all cybersecurity policies for the government; working closely with the Office of Management and Budget to ensure agency budgets reflect those priorities; and, in the event of major cyber incident or attack, coordinating our response.

To ensure that federal cyber policies enhance our security and our prosperity, my Cybersecurity Coordinator will be a member of the National Security Staff as well as the staff of my National Economic Council. To ensure that policies keep faith with our fundamental values, this office will also include an official with a portfolio specifically dedicated to safeguarding the privacy and civil liberties of the American people.

There's much work to be done, and the report we're releasing today outlines a range of actions that we will pursue in five key areas.

First, working in partnership with the communities represented here today, we will develop a new comprehensive strategy to secure America's information and communications networks. To ensure a coordinated approach across government, my Cybersecurity Coordinator will work closely with my Chief Technology Officer, Aneesh Chopra, and my Chief Information Officer, Vivek Kundra. To ensure accountability in federal agencies, cybersecurity will be designated as one of my key management priorities. Clear milestones and performances metrics will measure progress. And as we develop our strategy, we will be open and transparent, which is why you'll find today's report and a wealth of related information on our Web site, www.whitehouse.gov.

Second, we will work with all the key players -- including state and local governments and the private sector -- to ensure an organized and unified response to future cyber incidents. Given the enormous damage that can be caused by even a single cyber attack, ad hoc responses will not do. Nor is it sufficient to simply strengthen our defenses after incidents or attacks occur. Just as we do for natural disasters, we have to have plans and resources in place beforehand -- sharing information, issuing warnings and ensuring a coordinated response.

Third, we will strengthen the public/private partnerships that are critical to this endeavor. The vast majority of our critical information infrastructure in the United States is owned and operated by the private sector. So let me be very clear: My administration will not dictate security standards for private companies. On the contrary, we will collaborate with industry to find technology solutions that ensure our security and promote prosperity.

Fourth, we will continue to invest in the cutting-edge research and development necessary for the innovation and discovery we need to meet the digital challenges of our time. And that's why my administration is making major investments in our information infrastructure: laying broadband lines to every corner of America; building a smart electric grid to deliver energy more efficiently; pursuing a next generation of air traffic control systems; and moving to electronic health records, with privacy protections, to reduce costs and save lives.

And finally, we will begin a national campaign to promote cybersecurity awareness and digital literacy from our boardrooms to our classrooms, and to build a digital workforce for the 21st century. And that's why we're making a new commitment to education in math and science, and historic investments in science and research and development. Because it's not enough for our children and students to master today's technologies -- social networking and e-mailing and texting and blogging -- we need them to pioneer the technologies that will allow us to work effectively through these new media and allow us to prosper in the future. So these are the things we will do.

Let me also be clear about what we will not do. Our pursuit of cybersecurity will not -- I repeat, will not include -- monitoring private sector networks or Internet traffic. We will preserve and protect the personal privacy and civil liberties that we cherish as Americans. Indeed, I remain firmly committed to net neutrality so we can keep the Internet as it should be -- open and free.

The task I have described will not be easy. Some 1.5 billion people around the world are already online, and more are logging on every day. Groups and governments are sharpening their cyber capabilities. Protecting our prosperity and security in this globalized world is going to be a long, difficult struggle demanding patience and persistence over many years.

But we need to remember: We're only at the beginning. The epochs of history are long -- the Agricultural

WHAT THE GOVERNMENT AND POLITICIANS SAY

Revolution; the Industrial Revolution. By comparison, our Information Age is still in its infancy. We're only at Web 2.0. Now our virtual world is going viral. And we've only just begun to explore the next generation of technologies that will transform our lives in ways we can't even begin to imagine.

So a new world awaits -- a world of greater security and greater potential prosperity -- if we reach for it, if we lead. So long as I'm President of the United States, we will do just that. And the United States -- the nation that invented the Internet, that launched an information revolution, that transformed the world -- will do what we did in the 20th century and lead once more in the 21st.

Thank you very much, everybody. Thank you. (Applause.)

1. In this speech, president Barack Obama discusses a need for better digital literacy. What does this mean to you?

2. President Obama also highlights how unprepared the United States is for cyberwarfare. Considering how long the internet has been a part of daily life, why do you think the US failed to plan for the attacks we now face? How can they get ahead of this for the future?

CHAPTER 3

WHAT THE COURTS SAY

Very little has been decided on cyberwarfare. The issue is so new that the courts have yet to tackle the problem head-on. In fact, most of the cases that have impacted cybersecurity and cyberwarfare so far have had little to do with war. Instead, the cases that are changing how we view cyberattacks have to do with everyday internet usage issues, from how search engines operate to what information suspected criminals are required to disclose to authorities while under investigation. As you'll learn from the following legal opinions and briefs, the law around the digital world is complex, and there is no easy answer to how to properly handle cybersecurity.

WHAT THE COURTS SAY

EXCERPT FROM *SPOKEO, INC. V. ROBINS*, FROM THE UNITED STATES SUPREME COURT, MAY 16, 2016

Justice Alito delivered the opinion of the Court.

This case presents the question whether respondent Robins has standing to maintain an action in federal court against petitioner Spokeo under the Fair Credit Reporting Act of 1970 (FCRA or Act), 84Stat. 1127, as amended, 15 U. S. C. §1681 *et seq.*

Spokeo operates a "people search engine." If an individual visits Spokeo's Web site and inputs a person's name, a phone number, or an e-mail address, Spokeo conducts a computerized search in a wide variety of databases and provides information about the subject of the search. Spokeo performed such a search for information about Robins, and some of the information it gathered and then disseminated was incorrect. When Robins learned of these inaccuracies, he filed a complaint on his own behalf and on behalf of a class of similarly situated individuals.

The District Court dismissed Robins' complaint for lack of standing, but a panel of the Ninth Circuit reversed. The Ninth Circuit noted, first, that Robins had alleged that "Spokeo violated *his* statutory rights, not just the statutory rights of other people," and, second, that "Robins's personal interests in the handling of his credit information are individualized rather than collective." 742 F. 3d 409, 413 (2014). Based on these two observations, the Ninth Circuit held that Robins had adequately alleged injury in fact, a requirement for standing under Article III of the Constitution. *Id.*, at 413–414.

This analysis was incomplete. As we have explained in our prior opinions, the injury-in-fact requirement requires a plaintiff to allege an injury that is both "concrete and particularized." *Friends of the Earth, Inc. v. Laidlaw Environmental Services (TOC), Inc.*, 528 U. S. 167 –181 (2000) (emphasis added). The Ninth Circuit's analysis focused on the second characteristic (particularity), but it overlooked the first (concreteness). We therefore vacate the decision below and remand for the Ninth Circuit to consider both aspects of the injury-in-fact requirement.

I

The FCRA seeks to ensure "fair and accurate credit reporting." §1681(a)(1). To achieve this end, the Act regulates the creation and the use of "consumer report[s]"[1] by "consumer reporting agenc[ies]"[2] for certain specified purposes, including credit transactions, insurance, licensing, consumer-initiated business transactions, and employment. See §§1681a(d)(1)(A)–(C); §1681b. Enacted long before the advent of the Internet, the FCRA applies to companies that regularly disseminate information bearing on an individual's "credit worthiness, credit standing, credit capacity, character, general reputation, personal characteristics, or mode of living." §1681a(d)(1).

The FCRA imposes a host of requirements concerning the creation and use of consumer reports. As relevant here, the Act requires consumer reporting agencies to "follow reasonable procedures to assure maximum possible accuracy of" consumer reports, §1681e(b); to notify providers and users of consumer infor-

WHAT THE COURTS SAY

mation of their responsibilities under the Act, §1681e(d); to limit the circumstances in which such agencies provide consumer reports "for employment purposes," §1681b(b)(1); and to post toll-free numbers for consumers to request reports, §1681j(a).

The Act also provides that "[a]ny person who willfully fails to comply with any requirement [of the Act] with respect to any [individual[3]] is liable to that [individual]" for, among other things, either "actual damages" or statutory damages of $100 to $1,000 per violation, costs of the action and attorney's fees, and possibly punitive damages. §1681n(a).

Spokeo is alleged to qualify as a "consumer reporting agency" under the FCRA.[4] It operates a Web site that allows users to search for information about other individuals by name, e-mail address, or phone number. In response to an inquiry submitted online, Spokeo searches a wide spectrum of databases and gathers and provides information such as the individual's address, phone number, marital status, approximate age, occupation, hobbies, finances, shopping habits, and musical preferences. App. 7, 10–11. According to Robins, Spokeo markets its services to a variety of users, including not only "employers who want to evaluate prospective employees," but also "those who want to investigate prospective romantic partners or seek other personal information." Brief for Respondent 7. Persons wishing to perform a Spokeo search need not disclose their identities, and much information is available for free.

At some point in time, someone (Robins' complaint does not specify who) made a Spokeo search request for information about Robins, and Spokeo trawled its sources and generated a profile. By some means not detailed in Robins' complaint, he became aware of the contents of that profile and discovered that it contained inaccurate information. His profile, he asserts, states that he is married, has children, is in his 50's, has a job, is relatively affluent, and holds a graduate degree. App. 14. According to Robins' complaint, all of this information is incorrect.

Robins filed a class-action complaint in the United States District Court for the Central District of California, claiming, among other things, that Spokeo willfully failed to comply with the FCRA requirements enumerated above.

The District Court initially denied Spokeo's motion to dismiss the complaint for lack of jurisdiction, but later reconsidered and dismissed the complaint with prejudice. App. to Pet. for Cert. 23a. The court found that Robins had not "properly pled" an injury in fact, as required by Article III. *Ibid.*

The Court of Appeals for the Ninth Circuit reversed. Relying on Circuit precedent,[5] the court began by stating that "the violation of a statutory right is usually a sufficient injury in fact to confer standing." 742 F. 3d, at 412. The court recognized that "the Constitution limits the power of Congress to confer standing." *Id.*, at 413. But the court held that those limits were honored in this case because Robins alleged that "Spokeo violated *his* statutory rights, not just the statutory rights of other people," and because his "personal interests in the handling of his credit information are individualized rather than collective." *Ibid.* (emphasis in original). The court thus concluded that Robins' "alleged violations of [his] statutory rights [were] sufficient to satisfy the injury-in-fact requirement of Article III." *Id.*, at 413–414.

We granted certiorari. 575 U. S. ___ (2015).

WHAT THE COURTS SAY

II

A

The Constitution confers limited authority on each branch of the Federal Government. It vests Congress with enumerated "legislative Powers," Art. I, §1; it confers upon the President "[t]he executive Power," Art. II, §1, cl. 1; and it endows the federal courts with "[t]he judicial Power of the United States," Art. III, §1. In order to remain faithful to this tripartite structure, the power of the Federal Judiciary may not be permitted to intrude upon the powers given to the other branches. See *DaimlerChrysler Corp. v. Cuno*, 547 U. S. 332, 341 (2006) ; *Lujan v. Defenders of Wildlife*, 504 U. S. 555 –560 (1992).

Although the Constitution does not fully explain what is meant by "[t]he judicial Power of the United States," Art. III, § 1, it does specify that this power extends only to "Cases" and "Controversies," Art. III, §2. And " '[n]o principle is more fundamental to the judiciary's proper role in our system of government than the constitutional limitation of federal-court jurisdiction to actual cases or controversies.' " *Raines v. Byrd*, 521 U. S. 811, 818 (1997) .

Standing to sue is a doctrine rooted in the traditional understanding of a case or controversy. The doctrine developed in our case law to ensure that federal courts do not exceed their authority as it has been traditionally understood. See id., at 820. The doctrine limits the category of litigants empowered to maintain a lawsuit in federal court to seek redress for a legal wrong. See *Valley Forge Christian College v. Americans United for Separation of Church and State, Inc.*,

454 U. S. 464, 473 (1982) ; *Warth v. Seldin*, 422 U. S. 490 –499 (1975). In this way, "[t]he law of Article III standing . . . serves to prevent the judicial process from being used to usurp the powers of the political branches," *Clapper v. Amnesty Int'l USA*, 568 U. S. ___, ___ (2013) (slip op., at 9); *Lujan, supra*, at 576–577, and confines the federal courts to a properly judicial role, see *Warth, supra*, at 498.

Our cases have established that the "irreducible constitutional minimum" of standing consists of three elements. *Lujan*, 504 U. S., at 560. The plaintiff must have (1) suffered an injury in fact, (2) that is fairly traceable to the challenged conduct of the defendant, and (3) that is likely to be redressed by a favorable judicial decision. *Id.*, at 560–561; *Friends of the Earth, Inc.*, 528 U. S., at 180–181. The plaintiff, as the party invoking federal jurisdiction, bears the burden of establishing these elements. *FW/PBS, Inc. v. Dallas*, 493 U. S. 215, 231 (1990) . Where, as here, a case is at the pleading stage, the plaintiff must "clearly . . . allege facts demonstrating" each element. *Warth, supra*, at 518.[6]

B

This case primarily concerns injury in fact, the "[f]irst and foremost" of standing's three elements. *Steel Co. v. Citizens for Better Environment*, 523 U. S. 83, 103 (1998) . Injury in fact is a constitutional requirement, and "[i]t is settled that Congress cannot erase Article III's standing requirements by statutorily granting the right to sue to a plaintiff who would not otherwise have standing." *Raines, supra*, at 820, n. 3; see *Summers v. Earth Island Institute*, 555 U. S. 488, 497 (2009) ; *Gladstone, Realtors v. Village of Bellwood*, 441 U. S. 91, 100 (1979) ("In no event . . . may Congress abrogate the Art. III minima").

To establish injury in fact, a plaintiff must show that he or she suffered "an invasion of a legally protected interest" that is "concrete and particularized" and "actual or imminent, not conjectural or hypothetical." *Lujan*, 504 U. S., at 560 (internal quotation marks omitted). We discuss the particularization and concreteness requirements below.

1

For an injury to be "particularized," it "must affect the plaintiff in a personal and individual way." *Ibid.*, n. 1; see also, *e.g.*, *Cuno, supra*, at 342 (" 'plaintiff must allege personal injury' "); *Whitmore v. Arkansas*, 495 U. S. 149, 155 (1990) (" 'distinct' "); *Allen v. Wright*, 468 U. S. 737, 751 (1984) ("personal"); *Valley Forge, supra*, at 472 (standing requires that the plaintiff " 'personally has suffered some actual or threatened injury' "); *United States v. Richardson*, 418 U. S. 166, 177 (1974) (not "undifferenti-ated"); *Public Citizen, Inc. v. National Hwy. Traffic Safety Admin.*, 489 F. 3d 1279, 1292–1293 (CADC 2007) (collecting cases).[7] Particularization is necessary to establish injury in fact, but it is not sufficient. An injury in fact must also be "concrete." Under the Ninth Circuit's analysis, however, that independent requirement was elided. As previously noted, the Ninth Circuit concluded that Robins' complaint alleges "concrete, *de facto*" injuries for essentially two reasons. 742 F. 3d, at 413. First, the court noted that Robins "alleges that Spokeo violated his statutory rights, not just the statutory rights of other people." *Ibid.* Second, the court wrote that "Robins's personal interests in the handling of his credit information are individualized rather than collective." *Ibid.* (emphasis added). Both of these observations concern particularization, not concreteness. We have made it clear time and time again that an injury in fact must be both concrete and particularized. See, *e.g., Susan B. Anthony List v. Driehaus*, 573 U. S. ___, ___ (2014) (slip op., at 8); *Summers, supra*, at 493; *Sprint Communications Co. v. APCC Services, Inc.*, 554 U. S. 269, 274 (2008) ; *Massachusetts v. EPA*, 549 U. S. 497, 517 (2007) .

A "concrete" injury must be "*de facto*"; that is, it must actually exist. See Black's Law Dictionary 479 (9th ed. 2009). When we have used the adjective "concrete," we have meant to convey the usual meaning of the term—"real," and not "abstract." Webster's Third New International Dictionary 472 (1971); Random House Dictionary of the English Language 305 (1967). Concreteness, therefore, is quite different from particularization.

2

"Concrete" is not, however, necessarily synonymous with "tangible." Although tangible injuries are perhaps easier to recognize, we have confirmed in many of our previous cases that intangible injuries can nevertheless be concrete. See, *e.g., Pleasant Grove City v. Summum*, 555 U. S. 460 (2009) (free speech); *Church of Lukumi Babalu Aye, Inc. v. Hialeah*, 508 U. S. 520 (1993) (free exercise).

In determining whether an intangible harm constitutes injury in fact, both history and the judgment of Congress play important roles. Because the doctrine of standing derives from the case-or-controversy requirement, and because that requirement in turn is grounded in historical practice, it is instructive to consider whether an alleged intangible harm has a close relationship to a harm that has traditionally been regarded as providing a basis for a lawsuit in English or American courts. See *Vermont Agency of Natural Resources v. United States ex rel. Stevens*, 529 U. S. 765 –777 (2000). In addition, because Congress is well positioned to identify intangible harms that meet minimum Article III requirements, its judgment is also instructive and important. Thus, we said in Lujan that Congress may "elevat[e] to the status of legally cognizable injuries concrete, de facto injuries that were previously inadequate in law." 504 U. S., at 578. Similarly, Justice Kennedy's concurrence in that case explained that "Congress has the power to define injuries and articulate chains of causation that will give rise to a case or controversy where none existed before." *Id.*, at 580 (opinion concurring in part and concurring in judgment).

Congress' role in identifying and elevating intangible harms does not mean that a plaintiff automatically satisfies the injury-in-fact requirement whenever a statute grants a person a statutory right and purports to authorize that person to sue to vindicate that right. Article III standing requires a concrete injury even in the context of a statutory violation. For that reason, Robins could not, for example, allege a bare procedural violation, divorced from any concrete harm, and satisfy the injury-in-fact requirement of Article III. See *Summers*, 555 U. S., at 496 ("[D]eprivation of a procedural right without some concrete interest that is affected by the deprivation . . . is insufficient to create Article III standing"); see also *Lujan, supra*, at 572.

This does not mean, however, that the risk of real harm cannot satisfy the requirement of concreteness. See, *e.g.*, *Clapper v. Amnesty Int'l USA*, 568 U. S. ____. For example, the law has long permitted recovery by certain tort victims even if their harms may be difficult to prove or measure. See, *e.g.*, Restatement (First) of Torts §§569 (libel), 570 (slander *per se*) (1938). Just as the common law permitted suit in such instances, the violation of a procedural right granted by statute can be sufficient in some circumstances to constitute injury in fact. In other words, a plaintiff in such a case need not allege any additional harm beyond the one Congress has identified. See *Federal Election Comm'n v. Akins*, 524 U. S. 11 –25 (1998) (confirming that a group of voters' "inability to obtain information" that Congress had decided to make public is a sufficient injury in fact to satisfy Article III); *Public Citizen v. Department of Justice*, 491 U. S. 440, 449 (1989) (holding that two advocacy organizations' failure to obtain information subject to disclosure under the Federal Advisory Committee Act "constitutes a sufficiently distinct injury to provide standing to sue").

In the context of this particular case, these general principles tell us two things: On the one hand, Congress plainly sought to curb the dissemination of false information by adopting procedures designed to decrease that risk. On the other hand, Robins cannot satisfy the demands of Article III by alleging a bare procedural violation. A violation of one of the FCRA's procedural requirements may result in no harm. For example, even if a consumer reporting agency fails to provide the required notice to a user of the agency's consumer information, that information regardless may be entirely accurate. In addition, not all inaccuracies cause harm or present any material risk of harm. An example that comes readily to mind is an incorrect zip code. It is difficult to imagine how

WHAT THE COURTS SAY

the dissemination of an incorrect zip code, without more, could work any concrete harm.[8]

Because the Ninth Circuit failed to fully appreciate the distinction between concreteness and particularization, its standing analysis was incomplete. It did not address the question framed by our discussion, namely, whether the particular procedural violations alleged in this case entail a degree of risk sufficient to meet the concreteness requirement. We take no position as to whether the Ninth Circuit's ultimate conclusion—that Robins adequately alleged an injury in fact—was correct.

* * *

The judgment of the Court of Appeals is vacated, and the case is remanded for proceedings consistent with this opinion.

It is so ordered.

---

1. The *Spokeo* case questions whether harm caused by something intangible—like information on the internet—is the same as physical harm. Based on this case and what you know about the prevalence of the internet, do you think that harm caused online can be considered equivalent to physical harm experienced by victims?

"RULE 41 CHANGES ENSURE A JUDGE MAY CONSIDER WARRANTS FOR CERTAIN REMOTE SEARCHES," BY ASSISTANT ATTORNEY GENERAL LESLIE R. CALDWELL OF THE CRIMINAL DIVISION, FROM THE UNITED STATES DEPARTMENT OF JUSTICE, JUNE 20, 2016

Congress is currently considering proposed amendments to Rule 41, which are scheduled to take effect on Dec. 1, 2016.

This marks the end of a three-year deliberation process, which included extensive written comments and public testimony. After hearing the public's views, the federal judiciary's Advisory Committee on the Federal Rules of Criminal Procedure, which includes federal and state judges, law professors, attorneys in private practice and others in the legal community, rejected criticisms of the proposal as misinformed and approved the amendments. The amendments were then considered and unanimously approved by the Standing Committee on Rules and the Judicial Conference, and adopted by the U.S. Supreme Court.

The amendments do not change any of the traditional protections and procedures under the Fourth Amendment, such as the requirement that the government establish probable cause. Rather, the amendments would merely ensure that at least one court is available to consider whether a particular warrant application comports with the Fourth Amendment.

WHAT THE COURTS SAY

The amendments would not authorize the government to undertake any search or seizure or use any remote search technique, whether inside or outside the United States, that is not already permitted under current law. The use of remote searches is not new and warrants for remote searches are currently issued under Rule 41. In addition, most courts already permit the search of multiple computers pursuant to a single warrant so long as necessary legal requirements are met.

The amendments would apply in two narrow circumstances:

First, where a suspect has hidden the location of his or her computer using technological means, the changes to Rule 41 would ensure that federal agents know which judge to go to in order to apply for a warrant. For example, if agents are investigating criminals who are sexually exploiting children and uploading videos of that exploitation for others to see—but concealing their locations through anonymizing technology—agents will be able to apply for a search warrant to discover where they are located. A recent investigation that utilized this type of search warrant identified dozens of children who suffered sexual abuse at the hands of the offenders. While some federal courts hearing cases arising from this investigation have upheld the warrant as lawful, others have ordered the suppression of evidence based solely on the lack of clear venue in the current version of the rule.

And second, where the crime involves criminals hacking computers located in five or more different judicial districts, the changes to Rule 41 would ensure that federal agents may identify one judge to review an application for a search warrant rather than be required to submit separate warrant applications in each district—up to 94—where a computer is affected. For example, agents may seek a search warrant to assist in the investigation of a ransomware scheme facilitated by a botnet that enables criminals abroad to extort thousands of Americans. Absent the amendments, the requirement to obtain up to 94 simultaneous search warrants may prevent investigators from taking needed action to liberate computers infected with malware. This change would not permit indiscriminate surveillance of thousands of victim computers—that is against the law now and it would continue to be prohibited if the amendment goes into effect.

These changes would ensure a court-supervised framework through which law enforcement can successfully investigate and prosecute these instances of cybercrime.

1. The new rules noted by the Department of Justice say that law enforcement officers still need a warrant if they want to do a search of a suspect's digital files, even if that search will occur remotely. Why is it important for the courts to spell out this rule? What do you think the consequences would be if remote digital searches were allowed without a warrant?

2. The rules say that law enforcement agencies can use a warrant to search one computer or many

WHAT THE COURTS SAY

> computers if those computers are connected in an illegal scheme, because getting warrants for each computer or network involved would take too much time and could get in the way of justice being done. Do you think this contradicts the rule that a warrant is always needed? Why or why not?

EXCERPT FROM *UNITED STATES OF AMERICA V. APPLE MACPRO COMPUTER, ET AL.*, BY JUDGE THOMAS I. VANASKIE, FROM THE UNITED STATES COURT OF APPEALS FOR THE THIRD CIRCUIT, SEPTEMBER 7, 2016

This appeal concerns the Government's ability to compel the decryption of digital devices when the Government seizes those devices pursuant to a valid search warrant. The District Court found Appellant John Doe in civil contempt for refusing to comply with an order issued pursuant to the All Writs Act, 28 U.S.C. § 1651, which required him to produce several seized devices in a fully unencrypted state. Doe contends that the court did not have subject matter jurisdiction to issue the order and that the order itself violates his Fifth Amendment privilege against self-incrimination. For the reasons that follow, we will affirm the District Court's order.

CRITICAL PERSPECTIVES ON CYBERWARFARE

I.

During an investigation into Doe's access to child pornography over the internet, the Delaware County Criminal Investigations Unit executed a valid search warrant at Doe's residence. During the search, officers seized an Apple iPhone 5S and an Apple Mac Pro Computer with two attached Western Digital External Hard Drives, all of which had been protected with encryption software.[1] Police subsequently seized a password-protected Apple iPhone 6 Plus as well.

Agents from the Department of Homeland Security then applied for a federal search warrant to examine the seized devices. Doe voluntarily provided the password for the Apple iPhone 5S, but refused to provide the passwords to decrypt the Apple Mac Pro computer or the external hard drives. Despite Doe's refusal, forensic analysts discovered the password to decrypt the Mac Pro Computer, but could not decrypt the external hard drives. Forensic examination of the Mac Pro revealed an image of a pubescent girl in a sexually provocative position and logs showing that the Mac Pro had been used to visit sites with titles common in child exploitation, such as "toddler_cp," "lolicam," "tor-childporn," and "pthc."[2] (App. 39.) The Forensic examination also disclosed that Doe had downloaded thousands of files known by their "hash" values to be child pornography.[3] The files, however, were not on the Mac Pro, but instead had been stored on the encrypted external hard drives. Accordingly, the files themselves could not be accessed.

As part of their investigation, the Delaware County law enforcement officers also interviewed Doe's sister, who had lived with Doe during 2015. She related that Doe had shown her hundreds of images of child pornography on the encrypted external hard drives. She told the investigators that the external hard drives included "videos of children who were nude and engaged in sex acts with other children." (App. 40.) Doe provided the password to access the iPhone 6 Plus, but did not grant access to an application on the phone which contained additional encrypted information. Forensic analysts concluded that the phone's encrypted database contained approximately 2,015 image and video files.

On August 3, 2015, upon application of the Government, a Magistrate Judge issued an order pursuant to the All Writs Act requiring Doe to produce his iPhone 6 Plus, his Mac Pro computer, and his two attached external hard drives in a fully unencrypted state (the "Decryption Order"). Doe did not appeal the Decryption Order. Instead, he filed with the Magistrate Judge a motion to quash the Government's application to compel decryption, arguing that his act of decrypting the devices would violate his Fifth Amendment privilege against self-incrimination.

On August 27, 2015, the Magistrate Judge denied Doe's Motion to Quash and directed Doe to fully comply with the Decryption Order (the "Quashal Denial"). The Magistrate Judge acknowledged Doe's Fifth Amendment objection but held that, because the Government possessed Doe's devices and knew that their contents included child pornography, the act of decrypting the devices would not be testimonial for purposes of the Fifth Amendment privilege against self-incrimination. The Quashal Denial stated that a failure to file timely objections could result in the waiver of appellate rights. Doe did not file any objections to the Quashal Denial and did not seek review by way of appeal, writ of mandamus, or otherwise.

Approximately one week after the Quashal Denial, Doe and his counsel appeared at the Delaware County Police Department for the forensic examination of his devices. Doe produced the Apple iPhone 6 Plus, including the files on the secret application, in a fully unencrypted state by entering three separate passwords on the device. The phone contained adult pornography, a video of Doe's four-year-old niece in which she was wearing only her underwear, and approximately twenty photographs which focused on the genitals of Doe's six-year-old niece. Doe, however, stated that he could not remember the passwords necessary to decrypt the hard drives and entered several incorrect passwords during the forensic examination. The Government remains unable to view the decrypted content of the hard drives without his assistance.

Following the forensic examination, the Magistrate Judge granted the Government's Motion for Order to Show Cause Why Doe Should Not Be Held in Contempt, finding that Doe willfully disobeyed and resisted the Decryption Order. Based on the evidence presented at the hearing, the Magistrate Judge found that Doe remembered the passwords needed to decrypt the hard drives but chose not to reveal them because of the devices' contents. The Magistrate Judge ordered Doe to appear before the District Court to show cause as to why he should not be held in civil contempt.

On September 30, 2015, after a hearing, the District Court granted the Government's motion to hold Doe in civil contempt. On October 5, 2015, the District Court issued a "Supplemental Order to articulate the reasons for its

September 30th Order." (App. at 12.) The District Court noted that the Government's prima facie case of contempt was largely, if not entirely, uncontested. While the Government presented several witnesses to support its motion, Doe neither testified nor called witnesses. He offered no physical or documentary evidence into the record and provided no explanation for his failure to comply with the Decryption Order. The District Court remanded Doe to the custody of the United States Marshals to be incarcerated until he fully complies with the Decryption Order. This timely appeal followed.

II.

We have appellate jurisdiction under 28 U.S.C. § 1291. We ordinarily exercise plenary review over the District Court's authority to issue an order pursuant to the All Writs Act, *Grider v. Keystone Health Plan Cent., Inc.*, 500 F.3d 322, 327 (3d Cir. 2007), and "review a district court's decision on a motion for contempt for abuse of discretion." *Marshak v. Treadwell*, 595 F.3d 478, 485 (3d Cir. 2009). However, when the party seeking review has failed to preserve the issue in the trial court, we review only for plain error. See *Brightwell v. Lehman*, 637 F.3d 187, 193 (3d Cir. 2011); *Nara v. Frank*, 488 F.3d 187, 194 (3d Cir. 2007). We nonetheless exercise plenary review over challenges concerning subject matter jurisdiction. *United States v. Merlino*, 785 F.3d 79, 82 (3d Cir. 2015).

III.

Doe raises two primary arguments as to why he should not be held in contempt. First, he asserts that the District Court lacked subject matter jurisdiction to issue the Decryption Order under the All Writs Act. Thus, he argues that he is not in contempt of any valid order and the judgment of contempt must be vacated. Second, Doe contends that the Decryption Order violates his Fifth Amendment privilege against self-incrimination.

A.

Doe's first challenge concerns the All Writs Act, which permits federal courts to "issue all writs necessary or appropriate in aid of their respective jurisdictions and agreeable to the usages and principles of law." 28 U.S.C. § 1651(a). The All Writs Act does not itself confer any subject matter jurisdiction, but rather only allows a federal court to issue writs "in aid of" its existing jurisdiction. *Clinton v. Goldsmith*, 526 U.S. 529, 534 (1999); *Sygenta Crop Prot., Inc. v. Henson*, 537 U.S. 28, 31 (2002); *see also In re Arunachalum*, 812 F.3d 290, 292 (3d Cir. 2016) (per curiam). Therefore, a court has subject matter jurisdiction over an application for an All Writs Act order only when it has subject matter jurisdiction over the underlying order that the All Writs Act order is intended to effectuate. Additionally, a federal court may only issue an All Writs Act order "as may be necessary or appropriate to effectuate and prevent the frustration of orders it has previously issued in its exercise of jurisdiction otherwise obtained." *United States v. N.Y. Tel. Co.*, 434 U.S. 159, 172 (1977).

    Doe contends that the Magistrate Judge did not have subject matter jurisdiction to issue the Decryption Order because the Government should have compelled his compliance by means of the grand jury procedure and

WHAT THE COURTS SAY

not the All Writs Act. The grand jury process, however, is not the exclusive means by which the Government may collect evidence prior to indictment. See *Zurcher v. Stanford Daily*, 436 U.S. 547, 559 (1978) (allowing the Government to proceed by search warrant despite insistence that the investigation should proceed by subpoena); *United States v. Educ. Dev. Network Corp.*, 884 F.2d 737, 743 (3d Cir. 1989) (rejecting the argument that the Government could not obtain evidence by means of a search warrant and must proceed solely by grand jury). Here, the Magistrate Judge had subject matter jurisdiction under Federal Rule of Criminal Procedure 41 to issue a search warrant[4] and therefore had jurisdiction to issue an order under the All Writs Act that sought "to effectuate and prevent the frustration" of that warrant. *United States v. N.Y. Tel. Co.*, 434 U.S. 159, 172 (1977).

In arguing that the Magistrate Judge did not have subject matter jurisdiction to issue the Decryption Order, Doe also challenges the merits of that order, contending that it was not a "necessary and appropriate means" of effectuating the original warrant as required by the Supreme Court in New York Telephone. A contempt proceeding, however, generally "'does not open to reconsideration the legal or factual basis of the order alleged to have been disobeyed.'"[5] *United States vs. Rylander*, 460 U.S. 752, 756 (1983) (quoting Maggio v. Zeitz, 333 U.S. 56, 69 (1948)); *In re Contemporary Apparel, Inc.*, 488 F.2d 794, 798 (3d Cir. 1973) (same). Furthermore, Doe did not argue in the District Court that the Decryption Order was not an appropriate exercise of authority under the All Writs Act. Thus, even if the propriety of the Decryption Order was before us, our review would be

123

limited to plain error. *Brightwell*, 637 F.3d at 193. Under this framework, an appellant must show four elements: "(1) there is an 'error'; (2) the error is 'clear or obvious, rather than subject to reasonable dispute'; (3) the error 'affected the appellant's substantial rights, which in the ordinary case means' it 'affected the outcome of the district court proceedings'; and (4) 'the error seriously affect[s] the fairness, integrity or public reputation of judicial proceedings.'" *United States v. Marcus*, 560 U.S. 258, 262 (2010) (quoting *Puckett v. United States*, 556 U.S. 129, 135 (2009)).

In *New York Telephone*, the district court had issued an order authorizing federal agents to install pen registers in two telephones and directed the New York Telephone Company to furnish "all information, facilities and technical assistance" necessary to accomplish the installation. *N.Y. Tel. Co.*, 434 U.S. at 161. The Company argued that neither Fed. R. Crim. P. 41 nor the All Writs Act "provided any basis for such an order." *Id.* at 163. The Supreme Court, however, found that this order was "clearly authorized by the All Writs Act" as a necessary and appropriate means of effectuating the installation of the pen registers. *Id.* at 172.

Here, the Magistrate Judge issued a search warrant for the devices seized at Doe's residence. When law enforcement could not decrypt the contents of those devices, and Doe refused to comply, the Magistrate Judge issued the Decryption Order pursuant to the All Writs Act. The Decryption Order required Doe to "assist the Government in the execution of the...search warrant" by producing his devices in "a fully unencrypted state." As was the case in *New York Telephone*, the Decryption Order here was a necessary and appropriate means of effectuating the original search warrant.

WHAT THE COURTS SAY

Doe asserts that *New York Telephone* should not apply because the All Writs Act order in that case compelled a third party to assist in the execution of that warrant, and not the target of the government investigation. The Supreme Court explained, however, that the Act extends to anyone "in a position to frustrate the implementation of a court order or the proper administration of justice" as long as there are "appropriate circumstances" for doing so. *Id.* at 174. Here, as in *New York Telephone*: (1) Doe is not "far removed from the underlying controversy;" (2) "compliance with [the Decryption Order] require[s] minimal effort;" and (3) "without [Doe's] assistance there is no conceivable way in which the [search warrant] authorized by the District Court could [be] successfully accomplished." *Id.* at 174-175. Accordingly, the Magistrate Judge did not plainly err in issuing the Decryption Order.

B.

Doe also contends that the Decryption Order violates his Fifth Amendment privilege against self-incrimination and that this challenge is subject to plenary review. Doe raised a Fifth Amendment challenge in his Motion to Quash the Decryption Order. The Magistrate Judge denied that challenge, rejecting the argument that Doe's Fifth Amendment privilege would be violated. Doe did not file objections to that order, nor did he seek review by way of appeal, writ of mandamus or otherwise, despite the Quashal Denial order informing Doe that failure to file a timely objection may constitute a waiver of appellate rights. Doe also did not renew this self-incrimination claim during the contempt proceedings before the Magistrate Judge and the District Judge.[6] Instead, Doe only reasserted his Fifth Amendment claim in this appeal.

While Doe persists that his challenge to the contempt order entitles him to plenary consideration of the Fifth Amendment issue, we disagree. As noted above, it is generally the case that "a contempt proceeding does not open to reconsideration the legal or factual basis of the order alleged to have been disobeyed." *Rylander*, 460 U.S. at 756 (internal quotation marks and citation omitted).

Even if we could assess the Fifth Amendment decision of the Magistrate Judge, our review would be limited to plain error. *See United States v. Schwartz*, 446 F.2d 571, 576 (3d Cir. 1971) (applying plain error review to unpreserved claim of violation of privilege against self-incrimination). Doe's arguments fail under this deferential standard of review.

The Fifth Amendment states that "[n]o person...shall be compelled in any criminal case to be a witness against himself." U.S. CONST. amend. V. The Fifth Amendment, however, "does not independently proscribe the compelled production of every sort of incriminating evidence but applies only when the accused is compelled to make a Testimonial Communication that is incriminating." *Fisher v. United States*, 425 U.S. 391, 408 (1976). To be testimonial, a communication must either "explicitly or implicitly . . . relate a factual assertion or disclose information." *Doe v. United States*, 487 U.S. 201, 210 (1988).

The Supreme Court has recognized that in some instances, the production of evidence can implicate the Fifth Amendment. In *Fisher*, the Court stated that "[t]he act of producing evidence in response to a subpoena . . . has communicative aspects of its own, wholly aside from the contents of the papers produced." 425 U.S. at 410. The Court reasoned that compliance with a request for evidence may "tacitly concede[ ] the existence of the documents demanded and their possession and control by the [defendant]." *Id.* By "producing documents, one acknowledges that the documents exist, admits that the documents are in one's custody, and concedes that the documents are those that the [Government] requests." *United States v. Chabot*, 793 F.3d 338, 342 (3d Cir.), *cert. denied*, 136 S. Ct. 559 (2015). When the production of evidence does concede the existence, custody, and authenticity of that evidence, the Fifth Amendment privilege against self- incrimination applies because that production constitutes compelled testimony.

In *Fisher*, however, the Court also articulated the "foregone conclusion" rule, which acts as an exception to the otherwise applicable act-of-production doctrine. *Fisher*, 425 U.S. at 411. Under this rule, the Fifth Amendment does not protect an act of production when any potentially testimonial component of the act of production—such as the existence, custody, and authenticity of evidence—is a "foregone conclusion" that "adds little or nothing to the sum total of the Government's information." Id. For the rule to apply, the Government must be able to "describe with reasonable particularity" the documents or evidence it seeks to compel. *Hubbell*, 530 U.S. at 30.

Although we have not confronted the Fifth Amendment implications of compelled decryption, the Eleventh Circuit has addressed the issue and found that the privilege against self-incrimination should apply. In that case, a suspect appealed a judgment of contempt entered after he refused to produce the unencrypted contents of his laptop and hard drives. In *re Grand Jury Subpoena Duces Tecum*

Dated Mar. 25, 2011, 670 F.3d 1335, 1337 (11th Cir. 2012). The court found that "(1) [the suspect's] decryption and production of the contents of the drives would be testimonial, not merely a physical act; and (2) the explicit and implicit factual communications associated with the decryption and production are not foregone conclusions." *Id.* at 1346. The court reached this decision after noting that the Government did not show whether any files existed on the hard drives and could not show with any reasonable particularity that the suspect could access the encrypted portions of the drives. *Id.* Although the court did not require the Government to identify exactly the documents it sought, it did require that, at the very least, the Government be able to demonstrate some knowledge that files do exist on the encrypted devices. *Id.* at 1348–49.

Despite Doe's argument to the contrary, the Eleventh Circuit's reasoning in In *re Grand Jury Subpoena* does not compel a similar result here. In the Quashal Denial, the Magistrate Judge found that, though the Fifth Amendment may be implicated by Doe's decryption of the devices, any testimonial aspects of that production were a foregone conclusion. According to the Magistrate Judge, the affidavit supporting the application for the search warrant established that (1) the Government had custody of the devices; (2) prior to the seizure, Doe possessed, accessed, and owned all devices; and (3) there are images on the electronic devices that constitute child pornography. Thus, the Magistrate Judge concluded that the Decryption Order did not violate Doe's Fifth Amendment privilege against self-incrimination.

Unlike In *re Grand Jury Subpoena*, the Government has provided evidence to show both that files exist on the encrypted portions of the devices and that Doe can access them. The affidavit supporting the search warrant states that an investigation led to the identification of Doe as a user of an internet file sharing network that was used to access child pornography. When executing a search of Doe's residence, forensic analysts found the encrypted devices, and Doe does not dispute their existence or his ownership of them. Once the analysts accessed Doe's Mac Pro Computer, they found one image depicting a pubescent girl in a sexually suggestive position and logs that suggested the user had visited groups with titles common in child exploitation. Doe's sister then reported that she had witnessed Doe unlock his Mac Pro while connected to the hard drives to show her hundreds of pictures and videos of child pornography. Forensic analysts also found an additional 2,015 videos and photographs in an encrypted application on Doe's phone, which Doe had opened for the police by entering a password. Based on these facts, the Magistrate Judge found that, for the purposes of the Fifth Amendment, any testimonial component of the production of decrypted devices added little or nothing to the information already obtained by the Government. The Magistrate Judge determined that any testimonial component would be a foregone conclusion. The Magistrate Judge did not commit a clear or obvious error in his application of the foregone conclusion doctrine. In this regard, the Magistrate Judge rested his decision rejecting the Fifth Amendment challenge on factual findings that are amply supported by the record.[7]

Accordingly, Doe's challenges to the Decryption Order and Quashal Denial fail.

So, too, does Doe's challenge to the contempt order. At the hearing on the contempt motion, Doe maintained that he could not remember the passwords to decrypt the hard drives. In a civil contempt proceeding, when a defendant raises a challenge of impossibility of compliance, "the defendant bears the burden of production." *United States v. Rylander*, 460 U.S. 752, 757 (1983). At the contempt hearing, the Government presented several witnesses to support its prima facie case of contempt. Doe's sister testified to the fact that, while in her presence, Doe accessed child pornography files on his Mac Pro computer by means of entering passwords from memory. Further, a detective who executed the original search warrant stated that Doe did not provide his password at the time because he wanted to prevent the police from accessing his computer. Doe never asserted an inability to remember the passwords at that time. Doe presented no evidence to explain his failure to comply or to challenge the evidence brought by the Government. The District Court thus found Doe in contempt and ordered he be held in custody until he complies with the Decryption Order. The District Court did not abuse its discretion in finding Doe to be in contempt of the Decryption Order.

IV.

For the foregoing reasons, we will affirm the District Court's order of September 30, 2015 holding Appellant John Doe in civil contempt.

WHAT THE COURTS SAY

1. The court found that a suspect would not be incriminating himself if he helped law enforcement officials access digital devices or files that could contain incriminating evidence, and so giving an officer a password to unlock those files or devices would not violate the suspect's Fifth Amendment rights. Do you agree with the court? Explain.

2. When police obtain warrants to search suspects' homes or computers, the warrant spells out all the areas the police are allowed to search. If they find paperwork that support the claims against the suspect, it's very easy to know that because papers are easy to read. But digital files are harder to access at times. Do you think companies like Apple should be compelled by the law to unlock these files or devices if the suspect can't or won't? If yes, what do you think the negative impact of that would be? If no, do you think that would allow more people to get away with crime?

CHAPTER 4

WHAT ADVOCACY ORGANIZATIONS SAY

People who work in cybersecurity have a multitude of concerns when it comes to cyberattacks. There are those who want better security but fear that allowing the government to be involved in that security will lead to the creation of a surveillance state. Others believe that the only way to ensure our safety during a time of cyberwarfare is to allow the government to have access to everything digital, even if it does violate people's privacy. As you read the following articles, you'll be asked to consider what the authors think the future of cyberwarfare is, and whether you agree with their takes on what is and isn't acceptable or possible in the twenty-first century.

"RUSSIA'S AGGRESSIVE POWER IS RESURGENT, ONLINE AND OFF," BY FRANK J. CILLUFFO AND SHARON L. CARDASH, FROM *THE CONVERSATION*, AUGUST 25, 2016

The Bear is back. It's happening on the ground in and around Ukraine, inside the virtual inboxes of the Democratic National Committee and at American news organizations. Russian cyberattacks are yielding eye-popping headlines warning not only of a return to Cold War-style behavior, but of the relative decline of American capabilities and power.

The list of U.S. entities believed to have been breached by Russian hackers is long and troubling. It includes the White House, the State Department, the Defense Department, the NASDAQ stock exchange, the U.S. electrical grid and the Democratic National Committee. Russian cyberattackers have also attempted to hack the Moscow bureau of *The New York Times*.

As the targets have moved beyond U.S. government to key civilian institutions, there has been a good deal of speculation about possible motives. These range from a desire to influence the outcome of November's U.S. presidential election to the broader goal of undermining U.S.-European relations.

What do we know about Russia's capabilities, strategies and intents? And what should we know about this top-notch adversary, more advanced and stealthier than any other, so we can most effectively assess and address the prospect of a Russian threat?

A DEFT AND POWERFUL PLAYER

The United States remains a powerhouse of innovation and technological capacity. But the country is not alone when it comes to sophisticated tools and tradecraft in the cyber domain. Key players comprising Russia's "cyber arsenal" include Russia's foreign intelligence service (SVR), military intelligence agency (GRU), Federal Security Service (FSB), and Federal Protective Service (FSO).

Testifying before the U.S. Senate Armed Services Committee earlier this year, U.S. Director of National Intelligence James Clapper noted that Russia's cyberattacks are becoming more brazen, "based on its willingness to target critical infrastructure systems and conduct espionage operations even when detected and under increased public scrutiny."

Since the fall of the Berlin Wall, Russia's security and intelligence services have practiced the world's second-oldest profession using high-tech tactics. Years ago, Russia was quick to recognize and integrate the potential leverage that online tools and action could offer to military doctrine, strategy and operations. But recently Russia has been honing this model of war fighting, blending electronic and real-world power into a hybrid that is more than the sum of its parts.

The first lessons came from Russia's 2008 conflict with neighboring Georgia. By 2013, Valery Gerasimov, chief of the General Staff of the Armed Forces of the Russian Federation, was laying out the Russian military doctrine for the 21st century with emphasis on "nonmilitary means" (such as political and economic actions) supported by "concealed" military efforts (such as activities undertaken by special operations troops – or cyberspace operatives). Starting in 2014, that integrated approach was used in battle with Ukraine.

Attacks directed against the United States and other countries' governments and businesses have yielded economic and diplomatic secrets that serve to strengthen Russia's industries and negotiating hand in matters of trade and global politics. Put bluntly, stealing the results of others' research is faster and cheaper than investing oneself, just as knowing other players' cards makes deciding a poker player's next moves easier and more effective.

CONCEALING ITS TRUE MOTIVES

Russia makes extensive use of surrogates to further the country's objectives. These groups and individuals may be directly supported and sanctioned by the Russian state, or they may simply be operating at a level of remove that affords Russian officials plausible deniability. This in itself is not new: Russia has long relied on proxies to conceal its own hand and engage in deception – a practice known as "maskirovka." In the digital context, accurately identifying who is behind the keyboard is an ongoing challenge even for the most tech-savvy among us, though the U.S. and other countries are getting better at it.

Beyond identity, intentions are always tricky to establish correctly from the outside. Recall, for example, the Cold War practice of Kremlinology – analyzing the Soviet Union's government and policies to determine its future actions – which fell short of science even at the best of times. Some cases, however, are easier to analyze than others. For instance, Russian cybercriminals are assuredly motivated by

CRITICAL PERSPECTIVES ON CYBERWARFARE

the prospect of profits. But the lines between criminals and state-backed attackers are not necessarily well-defined; there have been reports about the convergence between the two groups in Russia — with this confluence serving to magnify the country's cyber capacity.

There are many reasons these manifestations of Russian capability and threat matter: They can destabilize countries and regions, and bring economic or even physical harm directly or indirectly to U.S. interests and those of our allies. These types of damage are real, if not always fully tangible.

Determined Russian propagandizing online has advanced narratives that seek to undercut "the institutions of the West" and spread social unrest in target countries. One method has been spreading fear of immigrants. In January 2016, Russian media outlets carried a fake story alleging a Russian girl had been raped in Berlin by a refugee.

Increasing our knowledge of Russia's capabilities, motives and intentions will allow us not only to deter attacks and respond to ones that happen, but also to act in ways that influence Russia's behavior toward outcomes the U.S. deems desirable. Today's digital threats are at once pervasive and profound, with no single defense or solution. We need more research into potential countermeasures tailored to specific adversaries if we are to thwart them and bolster U.S. national and economic security.

1. The author discusses all the different targets believed to have been hacked by Russian authorities. What are the dangers of a foreign agency hacking into a government office?

WHAT ADVOCACY ORGANIZATIONS SAY

2. A lot of the articles you've read so far focus on the negative impact of hacks like those perpetrated by Russia on the country and on the government. What do you think are some of the personal dangers of a country like Russia or North Korea hacking into American computers, be they government or corporate systems?

"CYBER ATTACKS TEN YEARS ON: FROM DISRUPTION TO DISINFORMATION," BY TOM SEAR, FROM *THE CONVERSATION*, APRIL 26, 2017

Today is the tenth anniversary of the world's first major coordinated "cyber attack" on a nation's internet infrastructure. This little-known event set the scene for the onrush of cyber espionage, fake news and information wars we know today.

In 2007, operators took advantage of political unrest to unleash a series of cyber measures on Estonia, as a possible form of retribution for symbolically rejecting a Soviet version of history. It was a new, coordinated approach that had never been seen before.

Today, shaping contemporary views of historical events is a relatively common focus of coordinated digital activity, such as China's use of social media to create war commemoration and *Russia Today*'s live-tweeting the Russian Revolution as its centenary approaches.

CRITICAL PERSPECTIVES ON CYBERWARFARE

In 2017 and into the future, it will be essential to combine insights from the humanities, particularly from history, with analysis from information operations experts in order to maintain cyber security.

ESTONIA GROUND TO A HALT

A dispute over a past war triggered what might be called the first major "cyber attack".

On April 27, 2007 the Government of Estonia moved the "Soldier of Tallinn" – a bronze statue that commemorated the Soviet Army of World War II – from the centre of the city to a military cemetery on Tallinn's outskirts. The action followed an extensive debate over the interpretation of Estonia's past. A "history war" concerning the role of the Soviet Union in Estonia during and after World War II had split Estonian society.

Several days of violent confrontation followed the statue's removal. The Russian-speaking population rioted. The protests led to 1,300 arrests, 100 injuries and one death. The disturbance became known as "Bronze Night".

A more serious disruption followed, and the weapons were not Molotov cocktails, but thousands of computers. For almost three weeks, a series of massive cyber operations targeted Estonia.

The disruption – which peaked on May 9 when Moscow celebrates Victory Day – brought down banks, the media, police, government networks and emergency services. Bots, distributed denial-of-service (DDoS) and spam were marshalled with a sophistication not seen before. Their combined effects brought one of the most digital-reliant societies in the world to a grinding halt.

WHAT ADVOCACY ORGANIZATIONS SAY

THE TALLINN MANUAL

In the aftermath, NATO responded by developing the NATO Cooperative Cyber Defence Centre of Excellence in Estonia. A major contribution of the centre was the publication of the Tallinn Manual in 2013 – a comprehensive study of how international law applied to cyber conflict. The initial manual focused on disabling, state-based attacks that amount to acts of war.

Tallinn 2.0 was released in February 2017. In the foreword, Estonian politician Toomas Hendrik Ives argues:

> *In retrospect, these were fairly mild and simple DDoS attacks, far less damaging than what has followed. Yet it was the first time one could apply the Clausewitzean dictum: War is the continuation of policy by other means.*

The focus of the new manual reveals just how much the world of cyber operations has changed in the ten years since Bronze Night. It heralds a concerning future where all aspects of society, not just military and governmental infrastructure, are subject to active cyber operations.

Now the scope for digital incursions by one nation on another is much wider, and more widespread. Everything from the personal data of citizens held in government servers to digitised cultural heritage collections have become issues of concern to international cyber law experts.

A DECADE OF CYBER OPERATIONS

In the ten years since 2007 we have lived in an era where persistent cyber operations are coincident with international armed combat. The conflict between Georgia (2008) and Russia, and ongoing conflict in the Ukraine (since 2014) are consistent with this.

These operations have extended beyond conventional conflict zones via intrusion of civic and governmental structures.

There are claims of nation-state actors active measures and DDoS incidents (similar to those that may have disabled last year's Australian census) on Kyrgyzstan and Kazakhstan in 2009.

German investigators found a penetration of the Bundestag in May 2015.

The Dutch found penetration in government computers relating to MH17 reports.

Now, famously, we know there were infiltrations between 2015-16 into US Democratic party computers. Revealed in the last few days, researchers have identified phishing domains targeting French political campaigns.

There are even concerns that, as Professor Greg Austin has explained, cyber espionage might be a threat to Australian democracy.

Recently, the digital forensics of a computer hacked in 1998 as part of an operation tagged Moonlight Maze revealed that it is possible that the same code and threat actor have been involved in operations since at least that time. Perhaps a 20-year continuous cyber espionage campaign has been active.

Thomas Rid, Professor in Security Studies at King's College London, recently addressed the US Select Committee on Intelligence regarding Russian active measures and influence campaigns. He expressed his opinion that understanding cyber operations in the 21st century is impossible without first understanding intelligence operations in the 20th century. Rid said:

> *This is a field that's not understanding its own history. It goes without saying that if you want to understand the present or the future, you have to understand the past.*

TARGETING INFORMATION AND OPINION

Understanding the history of cyber operations will be critical for developing strategies to combat them. But narrowly applying models from military history and tactics will offer only specific gains in an emerging ecosystem of "information age strategies".

The international response to the "attack" on Estonia was to replicate war models of defence and offence. But analysis of the last ten years shows that is not the only way in which cyber conflict has evolved. Even the popular term "cyber attack" is now discouraged for incidents smaller than Estonia, as risks on the cyber security spectrum have become more complex and more precisely defined.

Since Estonia 2007, internet-based incursions and interference have escalated massively, but their targets have become more diffuse. Direct attacks on a nation's defence forces, while more threatening, may in the future be less common than those that target information and opinion.

At the time, the attack on national infrastructure in Estonia seemed key, but looking back it was merely driving a wedge into an existing polarisation in society, which seems to be a pivotal tactic.

CRITICAL PERSPECTIVES ON CYBERWARFARE

Nations like Australia are more vulnerable than ever to cyber threats, but their public focus is becoming more distributed, and their goal will be to change attitudes, opinions and beliefs.

A decade ago in Estonia, a cyber war erupted from a history war. The connection between commemoration and information war is stronger than ever, and if nations wish to defend themselves, they will need to understand culture as much as coding.

1. The first major cyberattack against a government occurred in 2007. The author notes that this incident received little coverage and is not well remembered today. Based on what you've just read, why do you think this incident was forgotten? What do you think could be learned from this first cyberattack today?

2. The author says that it's impossible to understand twenty-first century cyberwarfare without first understanding the physical warfare of the twentieth century. What does this mean to you? How can understanding older methods help you understand what's happening today?

WHAT ADVOCACY ORGANIZATIONS SAY

"D.C. CIRCUIT COURT ISSUES DANGEROUS DECISION FOR CYBERSECURITY: ETHIOPIA IS FREE TO SPY ON AMERICANS IN THEIR OWN HOMES," BY NATE CARDOZO, FROM THE ELECTRONIC FREEDOM FOUNDATION, MARCH 14, 2017

The United States Court of Appeals for the District of Columbia Circuit today held that foreign governments are free to spy on, injure, or even kill Americans in their own homes--so long as they do so by remote control. The decision comes in a case called Kidane v. Ethiopia, which we filed in February 2014.

Our client, who goes by the pseudonym Mr. Kidane, is a U.S. citizen who was born in Ethiopia and has lived here for over 30 years. In 2012 through 2013, his family home computer was attacked by malware that captured and then sent his every keystroke and Skype call to a server controlled by the Ethiopian government, likely in response to his political activity in favor of democratic reforms in Ethiopia. In a stunningly dangerous decision today, the D.C. Circuit ruled that Mr. Kidane had no legal remedy against Ethiopia for this attack, despite the fact that he was wiretapped at home in Maryland. The court held that, because the Ethiopian government hatched its plan in Ethiopia and its agents launched the attack that occurred in Maryland from outside the U.S., a law called the Foreign Sovereign Immunities Act (FSIA) prevented U.S. courts from even hearing the case.

The decision is extremely dangerous for cybersecurity. Under it, you have no recourse under law if a foreign government that hacks into your car and drives it off the road, targets you for a drone strike, or even sends a virus to your pacemaker, as long as the government planned the attack on foreign soil. It flies in the face of the idea that Americans should always be safe in their homes, and that safety should continue even if they speak out against foreign government activity abroad.

FACTUAL BACKGROUND

Mr. Kidane discovered traces of state-sponsored malware called FinSpy, a sophisticated spyware product which its maker claims is sold exclusively to governments and law enforcement, on his laptop at his home in suburban Maryland. A forensic examination of his computer showed that the Ethiopian government had been recording Mr. Kidane's Skype calls, as well as monitoring his (and his family's) web and email usage. The spyware was launched when Kidane opened an attachment in an email. The spying began at his home in Maryland.

The spyware then reported everything it captured back to a command and control server in Ethiopia, owned and controlled by the Ethiopian government. The infection was active from October 2012 through March 2013, and was stopped just days after researchers at the University of Toronto's Citizen Lab released a report exposing Ethiopia's use of FinSpy. The report specifically referenced the very IP address of the Ethiopian government server responsible for the command and control of the spyware on Mr. Kidane's laptop.

We strenuously disagree with the D.C. Circuit's opinion in this case. Foreign governments should not

WHAT ADVOCACY ORGANIZATIONS SAY

be immune from suit for injuring Americans in their own homes and Americans should be as safe from remote controlled, malware, or robot attacks as they are from human agents. The FSIA does not require the courts to close their doors to Americans who are attacked, and the court's strained reading of the law is just wrong. Worse still, according to the court, so long as the foreign government formed even the smallest bit of its tortious intent abroad, it's immune from suit. We are evaluating our options for challenging this ruling.

1. According to the judgment cited by the author, a foreign country can spy on an American citizen on American soil and the citizen would have no way to demand recourse. The author says this is a bad decision and will harm our cybersecurity. Do you agree with the author? Why or why not?

2. The American government has been accused of spying on American citizens, most famously when Edward Snowden revealed the National Security Agency's PRISM program. Do you think that affected how the courts decided in the case of Ethiopia spying on American citizens? Do you think that makes the decision fair?

"THE COOLING WARS OF CYBER SPACE IN A REMOTE ERA," BY ESTHER KERSLEY, ALBERTO MUTI, AND KATHERINE TAJER, FROM *COMMON DREAMS*, NOVEMBER 7, 2014

Cyber space is a confusing place. As current discussions highlight the possibility of 'major' cyber attacks causing a significant loss of life or large scale destruction, it is becoming harder to determine whether these claims are hype or are in fact justified fears. A new report, published this week by VERTIC, commissioned by the Remote Control project, offers some clarity on the subject by assessing the major issues in cyber security today to help better inform the debate and assess what threats and challenges cyber issues really do pose to international peace and security.

HOW MUCH OF A THREAT ARE CYBER ATTACKS?

Cyber attacks have been identified as one of the greatest threats facing developed nations. Indeed, the US is spending $26 billion over the next five years on cyber operations and building a 6,000-strong cyber force by 2016 and the UK has earmarked £650 million over four year to combat cyber threats. This level of investment suggests that states view issues of cyber security as a question of national security. But how much of a threat do cyber attacks pose to national security and how much damage have they caused?

There is a need for caution when assessing the risk posed to national security by cyber threats. Indeed, although states are heavily investing in cyber security, to date, the majority of cyber incidents that have made the news have not directly impacted on a state's sovereignty, or threatened a state's survival. For that to happen, an attack would have to significantly affect a government's ability to control its territory, inflict damage to critical infrastructure or, potentially, cause mass casualties.

Nevertheless, some notable instances of cyber attacks have had a significant impact on international relations over the past decades. These are 'Stuxnet', the cyber attack targeting Iranian uranium centrifuges (allegedly launched by a combined US-Israeli operation), the 'Nashi' attacks on the Estonian government and private sector websites and web-based services, and the many instances of cyber-espionage that form the so-called 'Cool War' currently taking place between China and the US. Furthermore, cyber attacks have also been used as instruments of war in conjunction with conventional military operations, for example during the Russo-Georgian conflict in 2008 and most significantly during the Israeli air raid against a nuclear reactor facility in Syria in 2007.

However, to date no attack has led to largescale destruction or fatality, suggesting that the potential for this is unlikely. This is due to the great amounts of technological expertise, material resources and target intelligence required to carry out such an attack. These resources are currently only in the hands of states, that might hesitate in using cyber attacks in such a way, when other means are available. This could of course change, especially if different political actors acquired the necessary means.

WHAT SHOULD WE BE CONCERNED ABOUT?

This is not to say we have nothing to be concerned about. Although a largescale cyber attack that inflicts mass casualties is unlikely to occur in the near future, cyber activities can still affect civilian lives in other ways. The hyperbolic language used to describe the potential consequences of cyber attacks, combined with a lack of reliable, concrete information on the real risks posed by cyber threats has contributed to the 'securitisation' of the debate around cyber security issues. It is feared that this process will lead to possible dangers being overestimated, and vulnerabilities cast as national security threats of immediate concern. States' reactions to these perceived risks may cause negative implications on both citizens and international peace and security.

Already we are seeing a potential consequence of securitization as governments turn to surveillance as a preventative measure against cyber attacks. In addition, the difficulty of attributing cyber attacks, as well as the widespread fear that other countries will constantly engage in cyber espionage, has led some to claim that the 'cyber realm' favours the attacker. This, in turn, may lead states to engage in a 'cyber arms race', as well as foster a 'Cool War' dynamic of continuous attrition and escalation between states. This erosion of trust between states, as well as the diminishing of civil liberties, are two serious concerns with regards to the militarization of cyber space.

Cyber attacks also pose serious transparency and accountability issues due to the above-mentioned technical complexities of cyber attack attributions, as well as the ambiguous relationship between state and non-state actors (in the 'Nashi' attack in Estonia for example, the relation between the youth group responsible for the attack and the Russian government remains an ambiguous one). The lack of legal clarity in this area is also worrying, meaning attackers will often not face consequences for their actions.

The only existing international legislation in the field - the Budapest Convention - solely addresses cybercrime and no further issues (such as military use of cyberspace). The Convention also does not have enough support to provide enforcement of its objectives, has no monitoring regime and has not been signed by Russia or China. Furthermore, an attempt to set out 'rules' on the legal implications of cyber war - in The Tallinn Manual - found that the complexities of cyber conflict means there are many instances that do not easily adhere to current legislative standards. The speed of technology further hampers drafting of law and international legislation.

GROWTH OF REMOTE CONTROL WARFARE

The rise in cyber activities cannot be examined in isolation. Its growth is part of a broader trend of warfare increasingly being conducted indirectly, or at a distance. This global trend towards 'remote control' warfare has seen an increasing use of drones, special forces, private military and security companies as well as cyber activities and intelligence and surveillance methods by governments in the last decade.

Indeed the global export market for drones is predicted to grow nearly three-fold over the next decade, and a broader range of states are now using drones, including France, Britain, Germany, Italy, Russia, Algeria and Iran. The US has more than doubled the size of its Special Operations Command since 2001, and private military and security companies are playing an increasingly important role in both Afghanistan and Iraq, with over 5,000 contractors employed in Iraq this year.

The idea of countering threats at a distance, without the use of large military forces, is a relatively attractive proposition as the general public is increasingly hostile to 'boots on the ground'. However, the concerns highlighted in this latest report with regards to cyber activities are echoed in all 'remote' warfare methods as their covert nature means there are serious transparency and accountability vacuums.

As well as this, wider negative implications have been identified where these methods are in use, from the detrimental impact of drone strikes in Pakistan to instability caused by special forces and private military companies in Sub-Saharan Africa. The militarisation of cyber space is part of this growing trend and, like these other new methods of warfare, increased transparency and accurate information is essential in order to assess the real impact they are likely to have.

WHAT ADVOCACY ORGANIZATIONS SAY

1. The author says that cyberattacks so far have not actually threatened any country's sovereignty or caused casualties, and so they are not quite as big a threat as they're perceived. Do you agree with this point? List three reasons to backup your answer.

2. Cyberwarfare is not a singular activity, the author says—it needs to be considered alongside all the other ways we wage war. What are some ways that cyberwarfare enhances traditional methods of fighting wars? Are there ways you can think of that make cyberwar a less-preferable method of fighting?

CHAPTER 5

WHAT THE MEDIA SAY

The media has long been against cyberwarfare—or any war. When the United States went to war with Iraq in 2003, most news organizations came out as opposed to the war. The same is true of cyberwar. While many agree that the US having the ability to fight wars over the internet is good, they also fear what the government having that power means for everyone else—including news outlets themselves. There are fears of First Amendment abuses if the government can easily access anything they want through computers, and there's a fear that other countries having the ability to hack into our computers means they can attack not only government networks, but civilian networks as well. This chapter will explore what various media entities have written about cyberwarfare and what their opinions mean for how we think about the digital landscape in which we live.

WHAT THE MEDIA SAY

"AN ANONYMOUS HACKER MAY HAVE COMPROMISED JOHN KELLY'S CELL PHONE. IT'S ONLY A SIGN OF THINGS TO COME," BY JARED KELLER, FROM *TASK & PURPOSE*, OCTOBER 6, 2017

Trump administration officials "believe" that the White House Chief of Staff John Kelly's personal cell phone was "compromised" while he was serving as Secretary of Homeland Security, several anonymous U.S. government sources told Politico on Oct. 5. Although the White House claimed the former Marine general only used a secure work phone for government business (which, well, lol), those sources said Kelly "turned his phone into White House tech support this summer complaining that it wasn't working or updating software properly" — a period of time, officials fear, that "hackers or foreign governments may have had access" to sensitive data from Kelly's time as one of the nation's highest law enforcement officers, according to Politico.

Kelly's phone incident isn't the first time one of Trump's beloved generals has had his communications compromised, and given months of tension between Trump's coterie of West Wing loyalists and "Church Lady" (the nickname given to Kelly by some White House staffers), it would be easy to dismiss the report as internal jousting among batshit insane Trump sycophants. But there's actually a more logical explanation: Despite the insane fever swamps that threaten to distort legitimate reports of Russian hacking during the 2016 election, the country's army of hackers have targeted the cell phones of U.S. military personnel for years.

The day before news broke of Kelly's compromised cell phone, the *Wall Street Journal* reported that Western officials believe the Russian military is aggressively exploiting the personal smartphones of troops and politicians from NATO-aligned member nations, from the lowly combat troops deployed to Europe's Russian border this year to senior military and political officials. The goal of these electronic incursions, Western military sources told the *Wall Street Journal*, is "to gain operational information, gauge troop strength and intimidate soldiers."

Russia's electronic warfare capabilities have surged in recent years, from outfitting civilian cell phone towers and other civilian infrastructure with jamming devices to knock out incoming cruise missiles to disabling the electric grid for almost 250,000 Ukrainians amid increasing cyber weapon tests in the neighboring country. As recently as 2016, Russian GRU unit "Fancy Bear" used cell phone exploits to track the positions of Ukrainian D-30 towed howitzers that relied on an Android app for more efficient positioning. And in May 2017, Russia likely used Stingray communications intercept equipment — the equivalent of a "roving wiretap," as *TechDirt* wrote — to send threatening messages to Ukrainian troops about how their commanders will "find your bodies when the snow melts."

In recent months, Pentagon personnel deployed to NATO countries bordering Russia have experienced digital incursions first-hand. *The Wall Street Journal* described the experience of Lt. Col. Christopher L'Heureux, a 2nd Cavalry Regiment commander deployed to Poland to help train allied troops on their tactical response to a potential Russian invasion, who claimed he experienced a hack shortly after assuming command. As *The War Zone* points out, the Army's Asymmetric Warfare Group updated its "Russian New Generation Warfare Handbook" in 2016 detailing the various electronic and cyber warfare capabilities developed facing U.S. military personnel operating near Russia, including activities that closely resemble the experience of Ukrainian troops this past May.

So how did Russia-associated hackers go from targeting Army riflemen downrange to someone of Kelly's stature? There's an implicit assumption that the better the location of your office in the Pentagon's E-ring or at the State Department, the more secure your communications are. But if Hillary Clinton should have known better about using a private internet server during her time as Secretary of State and while Trump administration officials can claim ignorance over their own missteps, it's clear that Kelly, a career military man, should have known better when his phone started acting up back in December 2016.

But why can't DARPA or another agency whip up a specially designed secure smartphone like the one President Obama used to enjoy? Engineering a completely secure device like the spy-proof "blackphone" proposed by former Navy SEAL Mike Janke in March 2015 is a deeply flawed proposition. A 2009 DoD effort to engineer an encrypted mobile device cost more than $36 million over five years; according to Larson, "by the time it was ready for use, the carriers had upgraded to 4G networks with which it was incompatible." Not that compatibility would matter: An Army Capabilities Integration Center white paper published in 2016 found that not only do existing Pentagon policy and security constraints make developing a next-generation military smartphone cost prohibitive, but, in the case of the Army, would require "a radical change in how [the Department of

CRITICAL PERSPECTIVES ON CYBERWARFARE

Defense] and the Army protect its information from one of protecting the network to a philosophy" — a change the DoD simply doesn't seem poised to embrace on a large scale.

The federal bureaucracy may move slowly, but the Army already has its ass in gear to address the issue, a contrast that may make Kelly's hacking episode feel like a major violation to a retired Marine general who frequently patrols the perimeter of the White House. At least the *Washington Post* didn't publish his phone number.

"If lawmakers do not like the laws they've passed and we are charged to enforce—then they should have the courage and skill to change the laws," the retired Marine general said in his remarks on April 18 at George Washington University Center for Cyber and Homeland Security.

1. The author notes that even the military has trouble keeping up with how fast technology changes, which is part of why General Kelly's cellphone was able to be hacked in the first place. He discusses a number of options available to combat this problem. Of the solutions mentioned, which do you think is the most reasonable and most likely to be accomplished?

2. Why does it matter if military personnel or government officials have their phones hacked? What do you think are the negative consequences of such an action?

WHAT THE MEDIA SAY

"HOW SHOULD THE US RESPOND TO CYBER ATTACKS?" BY MICHELLE VILLARREAL ZOOK, FROM *TASK & PURPOSE*, JANUARY 13, 2015

GIVEN CYBER WARFARE'S INHERENTLY ASYMMETRIC NATURE, DO THE TRADITIONAL LAWS OF ARMED CONFLICT STILL HOLD TRUE?

The principles of *jus ad bellum*, the "right to war," and the laws of armed conflict have evolved through centuries of development and survived military innovations like aircraft and tanks. But given cyber warfare's inherently asymmetric nature and the difficulties in correctly and quickly attributing attacks, do the traditional laws of armed conflict still hold true? Or are we already living in an era where we hold one set of standards for countries that adhere to international law and a different set of standards for those countries that either encourage or ignore their citizens to participate in cyber attacks? Should we hold ISIS to the same set of standards for Monday's hacking of U.S. CENTCOM's social media pages as a state-sponsored group that hacks Sony?

The use of cyber militias is nothing new. Russia and China have tacitly encouraged the technique for the last decade deliberately in order to throw off attribution and save money (patriotic hackers who will work for free in their spare time are much cheaper than a military). The continuing questions over who really was behind the Sony hack will only further this behavior in that they encourage nation-states to utilize non-state actors to do their dirty work, knowing they can then be shielded by layers of doubt over identity. It's hard to retaliate if there's no return address on the malware or virus dumped onto your computer systems.

Countries like Russia and China utilizing civilian hackers to do their dirty work trigger a dilemma in distinguishing between combatants and non-combatants in a cyber world. Distinction between a lawful and unlawful combatant can be difficult enough in a face-to-face environment; imagine trying to figure it out in a virtual world just based on programming code or behavior. Are you dealing with a civilian hacker utilizing a coffee shop internet protocol address or a military hacker trying to utilize a civilian network? In a world where our networks are so intertwined, how does one distinguish between military networks and civilian networks in a retaliatory attack? Ideally, of course, a targeted attack would just take military resources offline while leaving hospitals and education facilities stable, but since any computer in the proper hands can be used to retaliate, any computer network can therefore be seen as a weapon by an attacking enemy. In the realm of cyber warfare, the distinction between lawful combatant and unlawful combatant and the distinction between a military network and a civilian network may become a luxury.

Cyber warfare can also cloud the principles behind proportionality in a military response. Here, again, Sony can be used as an example. An entity, rumored to be backed by North Korea, hacked a company doing business in America, potentially costing it billions of dollars (and a loss of prestige). If the United States government has a right to retaliate on Sony's behalf, what could it potentially do to North Korea to have any proportional

WHAT THE MEDIA SAY

impact? Sony likely has a greater gross domestic product than North Korea and North Korean civilians are unlikely to have any access to the Internet. But what if China was behind the attack, rather than North Korea, and to retaliate, the United States utilized the same distributed denial of service attacks on China that were rumored to have been used on North Korea? Suddenly the costs are astronomical to China's economy, dwarfing Sony's losses, and Chinese hackers launch their own retaliatory attacks. Imagine widespread distributed denial of service attacks in America, where we rely on the Internet for everything from banking to medical records, or what would happen if our power grids were hacked.

One thing that is indisputable is that virtual actions can have tangible, physical results. From the hack on Target last Christmas to the hack on Sony more recently, American companies and citizens are vulnerable. The United States government has been vague on admitting when a cyber attack constitutes an act of war — if it is true that the distributed denial of service attacks were retaliation for the Sony hack, why are we not pressing our Russian and Ukrainian allies more strenuously regarding the Rescator-backed hack on Target last Christmas?

The "International Strategy for Cyberspace" report, commissioned by the White House and released in 2011, will only go so far as to say that, "Consistent with the United Nations Charter, states have an inherent right to self-defense that may be triggered by certain aggressive acts in cyberspace," but then does not define what those "certain aggressive acts" might be. It's interesting, in theory, to ponder what self-defense measures could be triggered by a cyber attack, but it might not be theory

CRITICAL PERSPECTIVES ON CYBERWARFARE

within the next 10 years; not when technologies are growing exponentially year by year. A retaliatory distributed denial of service attack this year might become a complete shutdown of a power grid within five years.

Conflicts conducted in an entirely virtual realm — albeit with physical results — are a new arena in policy, giving the United States the potential to lead in establishing new doctrines and treaties, but in the meantime, leaving us in a world of nebulous unknowns, a sort of virtual Wild West that is open to exploitation and bad actors. Some of those bad actors will want to exploit our adherence to the rules and principles governing conflict in a physical realm, especially as we try to navigate what is essentially a new world and extrapolate laws and treaties to apply. The principles of jus ad bellum and the laws of armed conflict, then, must necessarily be as fluid and dynamic as the military conflicts and technologies they govern. We shouldn't get rid of them, but we should be prepared to adapt them for the cyber realm and the conflicts we will face there.

1. The author poses a question: If the US is allowed to act on behalf of companies hurt by cyberattacks from foreign actors, what constitutes a reasonable response from the US government? How would you answer that question? Should the US be able to respond to attacks on civilians if they are committed by non-government actors?

WHAT THE MEDIA SAY

2. In traditional warfare, civilians are considered neutral and cannot be targeted. However, as the author notes, many governments rely on civilian hackers to do their digital dirty work, making the line between civilian and combatant a bit blurry. How do you think civilian hackers should be treated if it appears they are acting on behalf of a government? Should they be considered civilians or soldiers? Explain your reasoning.

"NORTH KOREA: THE CYBERWAR OF ALL AGAINST ALL," BY JOHN FEFFER, FROM *FOREIGN POLICY IN FOCUS*, MARCH 14, 2017

The political theorist Thomas Hobbes warned in the 17th century that without the modern state and its sovereign control of territory, humanity would slip back into a state of nature in which violence was uncontrolled and ever-present. "A war of all against all" would break out, he wrote, in which neighbor would turn against neighbor. States would continue to fight one another, but a measure of stability would reign at the level of society.

Today, without any international authority to regulate cyberspace, a war of all against all has indeed broken out. Each day there are new headlines about a hacking scandal, a cyberattack against a bank or government institution, or even more serious offensive actions.

The United States pioneered this kind of warfare when, during the administration of George W. Bush, it inserted malware into the Iranian nuclear complex that destroyed centrifuges and set back the program. More recently, the United States was on the receiving end of cyberwarfare when hackers, probably at the behest of the Russian government, stole material from the Democratic Party, arranged for its release prior to the 2016 presidential elections, and influenced the outcome in favor of Donald Trump.

The latest revelations of cyberware, however, involve North Korea. *The New York Times* published an article on March 4 claiming that at least some of the many mishaps and failures associated with North Korea's missile program were the result of a secret U.S. program to thwart launches through electronic means.

This was not, in fact, the first admission that the United States had targeted North Korea through cyberspace. In late 2014, North Korea stood accused of hacking into Sony Pictures to discredit the film company around the time of its release of *The Interview*, which mocked Kim Jong Un. At the same time, however, came the revelation that the United States had been hacking into North Korea as early as 2010 and had installed malware that enabled tracking of some of North Korea's activities.

As I wrote at the time, "The Sony hack has been held up as an example of North Korea's specialty: asymmetrical warfare. It usually relies on the weapons of the weak against strong adversaries like the United States. But there was a dangerous symmetry lurking in the cyberworld all along. Spyware, it seems, is everywhere."

The latest information about U.S. attempts to disrupt North Korea's nuclear program carries with it several very important implications.

First, the Obama administration launched the initiative because it recognized that traditional missile defense was ineffectual. "Flight tests of interceptors based in Alaska and California had an overall failure rate of 56 percent, under near-perfect conditions," *The New York Times* noted. "Privately, many experts warned the system would fare worse in real combat."

Second, the cyberwarfare against North Korea has also basically failed. Despite the numerous failed tests, Pyongyang managed to put together a series of successful launches over the last year, including three medium-range rockets.

Third, cyberspace has become an increasingly dangerous place. Countries have developed the capacity not only to disrupt military operations but also to sabotage civilian infrastructure and paralyze an economy, as South Korea discovered in 2013 when an attack brought down several banks and broadcasters. This kind of warfare doesn't have any international rules of engagement, like the Geneva Conventions or what the United Nations has developed over the years.

Although Trump as candidate promised a new policy toward North Korea, his administration has so far responded to North Korea's nuclear program with more of the same. It has said that all options are on the table. It is moving forward with deployment of the THAAD missile defense system in South Korea. It has sent reassurances of support to Tokyo and Seoul. It is considering more sanctions and as well as placing North Korea back on the list of state sponsors of terrorism. It is waiting for China to do something.

What Trump hasn't done, however, is learn any lessons from the previous administration's cyberwarfare experiment. Missile defense doesn't work. The insertion of malware is only a temporary fix. The Obama administration at least showed that it could learn from its own failures by translating these lessons into a nuclear deal with Iran that has actually dealt with a potential proliferation threat through international cooperation.

It's time for the United States to apply the same lessons to North Korea. Negotiations and verifiable agreements are far more effective than threats and efforts at disruption.

And before cyberattacks truly spill out of control and the international community descends into a war of all against all, Washington should sit down with other countries to hammer out some rules of conduct. Otherwise, North Korea's nuclear program will be the least of our problems.

1. The author says that the US government needs to sit down and set down some rules of digital conduct to prevent all-out cyberwarfare. After reading this article and the others in the book, what do you think some of those rules should be?

WHAT THE MEDIA SAY

2. According to the author, the US is already at war with North Korea, at least online, but he believes this war can be halted, or at least cooled, if the two sides sit down to discuss the rules of cyberwarfare. Do you think this is a tactic that would work, knowing what you do about relations with North Korea? Why?

"CLAIMS OF US HACKING OF CHINA LEVELS THE MORAL GROUND —WHAT NEXT FOR THE CYBER WAR?" BY DAVID GLANCE, FROM *THE CONVERSATION*, JUNE 15, 2013

When US President Obama met with Chinese President Xi Jinping, he was planning to raise the thorny issue of China's alleged sustained hacking of US computers and ongoing theft of US intellectual property. The importance of the issue of Chinese hacking had been heightened in recent months with the escalation in reports of US businesses being hacked and having information stolen. As a consequence of this, the US Senate is considering a bill requiring the President to block imports of products that use stolen US technology or are made by companies implicated in computer theft. Exactly how these companies would be identified of course remains to be seen. But the point is that the hacking has become a central threat to the US across a broad range of fronts.

Any intention to raise this fully with the Chinese President however was completely undermined by the the revelations that the US have also been engaged in the systematic hacking of Chinese assets via their secret service surveillance program, Prism. Obama has subsequently tried to make a clear distinction between what he terms cyber attacks from China and what he believes the US is doing which is solely undertaking surveillance for counter-terrorism purposes.

Of course, this was all before NSA whistle-blower Edward Snowden revealed that in addition to the mass surveillance by Prism, the US had been directly hacking computers in Hong Kong and the Chinese mainland since 2009. Chinese targets allegedly included Chinese university and public officials.

Making matters worse are fears that Snowden will defect to China taking all of the other secrets he has accumulated from his time with the NSA. For NSA director General Alexander, there is a benefit in building up the case against Snowden by talking about the extreme harm he has created to US security by his revelations. Whether this is really the case will depend on the nature of the secrets Snowden had access to. So far, the revelations Snowden has made have been about what things have been done, rather than any specific details of how. For example, Snowden has talked in general terms of the US targeting "Internet routers" to give them access to "hundreds of thousands of computers". This information might allow the Chinese to re-examine the security of these routers and adopt defensive procedures against future attacks, but unless Snowden is also able to reveal exactly how these hacks worked, it gives the Chinese only a small advantage.

WHAT THE MEDIA SAY

In terms of how much Snowden's knowledge would help the Chinese, the question to consider is how much of this information do they already know? The Chinese have applied huge resources to building up their cyber security capabilities, for offense certainly but also likely for defensive strategies. They have also gained a huge amount of information through their hacking activities to date. According to one report since 2006, a single Chinese espionage group (PLA61398) has stolen hundreds of terabytes of data from at least 141 companies across 20 industries including aerospace and defence.

So would it come as a great surprise to the Chinese that the US have compromised network infrastructure or computer assets in Hong Kong and China? Probably not. The Chinese have claimed in the past that they have "mountains of data" concerning cyber attacks on China, many of which emanated from the US. It is likely that they are only too aware of the extent of the US's abilities in this area. Snowden's information might help in narrowing down the range of areas to focus on.

We are likely in the midst of a global Cyber War that is in essence a continuation of the Cold War. The potential military and industrial gains of cyber-espionage are so great that it is difficult to see any rationale for any country to stop engaging in it.

Before the secrets of Prism and Snowden's other revelations were made public, it was possible for the US to take the higher ground and make demands on China to act to curb the attacks. Since the revelations however, their position has been extremely weakened and any demands will just sound hollow. What this will mean is that countries will need to expend more money and resources on

CRITICAL PERSPECTIVES ON CYBERWARFARE

shoring up their defences with the expectation that the cyber attacks will not only continue, but will inexorably get worse.

Another question arising out of the ongoing exchange of cyber hostilities between the US and China is whether the US will eventually take steps to reduce its reliance on electronics and electronic products built outside of the US. As with the move to make the US less reliant on external sources of oil and gas, Obama and future presidents may decide that independence in the area of manufacturing vital electronics is even more important. This would have the effect of lessening the reliance on China even if it made these goods more expensive.

Whatever the path, it is fair to say that the relationship between China and the US will be tested in the coming weeks, especially if Snowden defects to China or is given safe harbour in Hong Kong. Whether China actually wants to accept Snowden if he decided to defect is another matter. Snowden might present the Chinese Government with more problems than any potential advantages. Both governments are perhaps wishing that they were living in less interesting times.

1. One of the questions the author brings up is that American tech products are largely produced in China, a country with which America currently has political tensions, and who is suspected to participate in cyberwarfare against its enemies. Do you think this is a problem for American cybersecurity?

WHAT THE MEDIA SAY

2. The author notes that there is a lot to gain from one country spying on another electronically, and very little to gain from stopping. What are some things that you think could convince countries to stop using digital espionage tactics?

"SHOULD CYBER WARFARE HAVE ITS OWN BRANCH?" BY CARL FORSLING, FROM *TASK & PURPOSE*, JUNE 28, 2016

IF CYBER WARFARE REMAINS JUST A NICHE WITHIN MILITARY SERVICES, THE U.S. WILL NEVER BE ABLE TO DEVELOP THE TALENTED WARRIORS IT NEEDS.

In 1947, the U.S. defense establishment finally recognized that airpower was an environment distinct and separate from sea or air. It required specialized knowledge and training, as well as a service culture that did not subordinate airpower to other functions within that service. The U.S. Air Force was created as a separate, independent service.

The other services retained air arms devoted largely to their respective tactical and operational needs, such as the Marine Corps' and Army's close-air support. The Air Force was responsible for the big picture, aviation in general

CRITICAL PERSPECTIVES ON CYBERWARFARE

support and for strategic airpower, including the nuclear bomber and intercontinental ballistic missile forces.

Those lines have been blurred, redrawn, and blurred again over the past half-century, but the paradigm has generally worked well. This was especially true during the Cold War, where air power from missiles and bombers was the center of gravity for the decades-long standoff.

In the 21st century, cyber warfare has become a center of gravity, especially in the operations-other-than-war which define today's multi-polar world. Wherever bullets and bombs aren't flying, electrons are. Though the U.S. never dropped bombs on Iran, it delivered a critical blow against its nuclear infrastructure by means of the Stuxnet computer virus. Similarly, enemies of the U.S. such as ISIS try to damage American interests by using cyberattacks. Just as airpower was during the Cold War, cyber warfare is becoming the instrument of perpetual standoffs between the U.S. and potential adversaries such as China and Russia.

With computers controlling everything from aircraft to the power grid, cyber is as important a battlespace as the air. It is similar to airpower in that it can't hold territory, but the country that controls cyber has a head start on owning the battlefield. Almost as important, the country that loses cyber loses the battlefield.

As much as I respect the soldiers, sailors, airmen, and Marines holding the fort down in the cyber battlefields today, we can't delude ourselves into thinking we're getting anywhere near the top performers in the field. The military has some of the toughest individuals in the country in its combat arms and special operations forces. It has some of the best pilots in the country flying its aircraft. But the nation's top young computer scientists are not swarming to the armed forces, despite some of the biggest bonuses in the military.

Why would they? While the military's system of starting at the bottom, doing scut work for years, and gradually working up a hierarchy is a great system for building the character and leadership needed to take a hill, but it's also not conducive to innovation in the way the computer science field typically operates.

The military services can attempt to change to accommodate this. The Army considered softening its fitness standards for cyber troops. Secretary of Defense Ash Carter is looking at allowing individuals to enter the military at high ranks. Much of his rationale comes from the need to get cyber warriors.

These are actually the exact types of things we need to do to enhance the nation's cyber warfare capability. Unfortunately, they will also induce much unnecessary friction and dissent in the ranks. An infantryman, or even a mechanic, is going to scoff at a cyber warrior. That's true even if he or she is winning an electronic war against China, if he or she is losing the war against Oreos working under reduced fitness standards. Similarly, a cyber warfare colonel is going to have some issues influencing his peers who hold more than 20 years of service over him or her, no matter how brilliant he or she is.

While these factors could be overcome in time, time is one thing we don't have in the cyber realm. While the services can maintain their individual cyber activities in support of tactical objectives, just as they do for aviation today, operational and strategic-level cyber warfare needs its own service.

As in the beginning of airpower, cyber warfare is at risk of being subordinated to individual services' interests instead of the strategic goals of the U.S. A standalone service would be better able to emphasize the unique capabilities of cyber warfare without the baggage of being one of many supporting element within the traditional services.

If cyber remains just a niche with those services, it will never have bonafide career paths for top individuals. A cyber warrior will never be, nor should be, the commandant of the Marine Corps or Air Force chief of staff, for example. The tactics and leadership necessary in cyber are distinct and different. This is true down through the ranks as well. Cyber is not just another support military job, like supply or maintenance. It is a significant weapon of strike and shield of defense in the U.S. arsenal.

In the information age, cyber can be just as deadly as a missile, and deserves a seat amongst top military commanders, at a minimum as a full unified command, and even better as a full member of the Joint Chiefs of Staff.

This service would be free to adopt the practices, tactics, and service culture that would support the cyber mission, and not have to fight through existing service bureaucracy. It would be able to fuse the military's enemy focus with the new practices and innovation needed in this new realm.

Cyber is already past where aviation was in 1947, and the U.S. is already behind in adapting its military cyber capability. We can't afford to lose the new digital Cold War against China and Russia any more than we could afford to lose the old Cold War against the Soviet Union.

WHAT THE MEDIA SAY

1. The author discusses how cyberwarfare is similar in many ways to air-based war. What are some of the reasons given? Do you agree that these two methods of fighting are similar? Explain.

2. The author notes that the military has considered changing standards for those who enter the cyber fighting force as opposed to the more traditional military forces, like the infantry. Do you think having different standards is a good thing? Do you think changing the rules for one part of the military would affect how well the cyber forces work with the more traditional military forces? Why or why not?

"GETTING 'CYBER' RIGHT FOR THE DEPARTMENT OF DEFENSE," BY GREGORY V. COX AND PRISCILLA E. GUTHRIE, FROM *WAR ON THE ROCKS*, NOVEMBER 9, 2017

"Cyber" is getting a lot of press these days. The problems seem endless, from nuisances, to hacks involving major corporations, to interference in democratic elections, to

CRITICAL PERSPECTIVES ON CYBERWARFARE

existential threats to the United States. The Department of Defense is clearly responsible for protecting against some of these threats, but where should the line be drawn? The answer, unfortunately, is unclear.

A good example of differing views on this question is the recent exchange between Sen. John McCain and Kenneth Rapuano, the assistant secretary of defense for homeland defense and global security. McCain believes the Department of Defense should have relatively broad cybersecurity responsibilities while Rapuano thinks its responsibilities should be defined more narrowly. Both gentlemen have valid bases for starkly different perspectives.

For example, Rapuano's view is statutorily supported by the *Posse Comitatus Act* that limits the military's role in domestic security matters. This act originated in 1878 when an overbearing militia could be easily imagined but cyber activities could not. And much more recently, the *White House Executive Order on Cybersecurity* delineated cybersecurity expectations for the Departments of Homeland Security, Commerce, Treasury, Justice, State, and others beyond the Department of Defense — cybersecurity is not just the Pentagon's problem.

Yet McCain observes that a primary Defense Department cyber mission is to "defend the nation against cyberattacks of significant consequence" and reasonable people could surely interpret that as protecting critical infrastructure, including political election processes. Why should the Defense Department shun responsibility for this?

We observe that even though the Pentagon has a long way to go to successfully confront its acknowledged cyber challenges, it — with significant help from the intelligence community — has the most capabilities within the executive branch for responding to cyber intrusions or attacks. Thus we propose that the Department of Defense should *show the way* toward a satisfactory approach that could then be adopted by other government departments and agencies.

POTENTIAL SCOPE OF THE PROBLEMS

Despite Pentagon definitions for *cyberspace, cybersecurity, cyberspace operations, cyberspace workforce*, and other related terms, its cyber responsibilities appear to be interpreted narrowly sometimes (even within Title 10 of U.S. Code). Narrow definitions naturally lead to narrow scopes of responsibility, reinforcing Rapuano's perspective.

But even within the Department of Defense, a recent Defense Science Board Task Force offered a broader interpretation of "cyber", emphasizing that even within the department's scope, cyber elements include more than just the computer networks but also software and hardware embedded in weapons systems, logistics and human resource systems, and infrastructure systems. A few hypothetical scenarios illustrate the board's point.

Suppose that one of the Navy's new *Zumwalt*-class destroyers, operating with an integrated control system for its engineering plant supporting its navigation and combat systems, became dead-in-the-water and had to be towed to a local port for repair. If, during those months-long repairs, it became evident that the ship was the victim of a sophisticated cyber attack to its engineering plant, what response would be appropriate?

CRITICAL PERSPECTIVES ON CYBERWARFARE

What if during the Army's attempt to launch a missile during a training event, the missile self-destructed shortly after launch, and a second launch attempt produced the same outcome? Suppose that subsequent investigation could not rule out the possibility that the software that altered the timing of sequential launch events had been infected. What should come next?

What if the military's logistics system abruptly canceled orders for some critical supplies and rerouted others in the midst of an overseas crisis? What should happen if an investigation discovered that relatively unsophisticated malware had been introduced into related software used by several key vendors?

These troubling scenarios are compounded because even though they would demand a purposeful response involving the Department of Defense, it isn't obvious which Pentagon official(s) should lead the response, or more importantly, take the steps to ensure that the attacks are not carried out in the first place. Where should the buck stop?

In the *Zumwalt* scenario for example, was the problem caused by an operator who failed to follow doctrine or training? Or was there a hardware or software deficiency behind the problem, perhaps a vulnerability that was exploited by an adversary? If so, were maintenance procedures at fault, such as a failure to install the latest software patch? Or was it a systemic vulnerability that testing and evaluation failed to identify? Perhaps the vulnerability wasn't even tested because the system's requirements did not stipulate the ability to withstand the problem. If that was the case, why should the program manager, or contractor, have allocated the resources

WHAT THE MEDIA SAY

necessary to develop the system for performance above and beyond its stipulated requirements? Could it be that poorly conceived requirements were validated by the Joint Requirements Oversight Council? Given the many years between the establishment of requirements and operational capabilities, the requirements may have been set a decade ago, before cyber vulnerabilities were as well understood as they are today.

But even though those scenarios involve attacks beyond traditional computer networks, they still conform to the Science Board's relatively broad view of cyber activities. We can offer additional scenarios that transcend that broad view and which would nonetheless affect the Department of Defense to some degree.

For example, what if several deep oil wells operating under U.S. leases in the Gulf of Mexico began to malfunction, causing limited spillage and otherwise becoming inoperable? Suppose that subsequent investigation in the operating software of nearby oil platforms revealed malware designed to cause similar effects? A temporary halt might be placed on all deep-well energy production as the problems are sorted out. Although nominally not a primary concern for the Department of Defense, it still represents an attack on the United States. And as the price for fuel begins to rise, the military must curtail some readiness training and exercises, thus the impact would be felt, perhaps severely.

Or what if a foreign entity were to create several fake (but credible) Facebook profiles for senior national security leaders, enabling it to gain background information on many other defense personnel that "friend" the leaders before the bogus sites are disabled? This would affect the Defense

Department, even though it might be a problem that should be solved by law enforcement or perhaps by the private sector.

Or what if a foreign entity posted a damaging "news item" concerning the Pentagon, maybe holding a grain of truth but is otherwise false, and employed auto-generating retransmissions of the news in an attempt to embarrass and distract Pentagon officials?

There are endless scenarios, and the correct answer to the question of where the Department of Defense's duties lie is probably to demarcate what's "in" and what's "out" of its set of responsibilities. The first three scenarios are clearly "in" under existing statutes, while the latter three may represent nuisances or problems for which the department has varying degrees of interest but no overall responsibility to develop or maintain capabilities.

Regardless of the Defense Department's demarcation, the U.S. government has vested interests in all of these scenarios and therefore the government needs a skilled workforce to address the broad array of concerns. The boundary between the Defense Department's cyber responsibilities and non-responsibilities might not be as significant if there was an adequate supply of skilled workers for the overall (government and private) cyber workforce, but there will be a shortage of cyber-skilled workers for the foreseeable future. This implies that workers who are engaged outside the Pentagon's core interests will not generally be available to support those interests.

IMPLICATIONS AND RECOMMENDATIONS

We appreciate that the cyber landscape, or perhaps more accurately our understanding of the cyber landscape, has evolved, so we should expect continued evolution of that understanding. But we have identified three fundamental problems here: unclear demarcation of Department of Defense cyber responsibilities, identification of the responsible (Pentagon) cyber officials, and a shortage of skilled cyber workforce competing with non-defense demands. To avoid playing a never-ending game of "catch-up," there are three steps the secretary of defense can take.

1. WORK TO ESTABLISH THE DEPARTMENT'S SET OF CYBER RESPONSIBILITIES SMARTLY.

Any potential future cyber event with significant implications for the department should fall within its set of responsibilities. The Pentagon's current definition of cyberspace appears too narrow, or at least appears to be interpreted too narrowly in practice, to accommodate all potential events, which may be why the Defense Science Board offered its expanded definition of cyber.

We recognize the difficulties in taking responsibility for "everything," but counter with the argument that everything of concern to the department needs to be unambiguously addressed somewhere. A risk assessment should address which portion of the demand for the cyber workforce can be sacrificed in the short term (while still acknowledging responsibility for it), and alternative technologies, strategies, and policies to mitigate the risk of these shortfalls can be devised. Without a comprehensive examination of the alternatives and exploration of mitigation approaches, the choices will be made implicitly if not deliberately. Explicitly focusing on these choices, with a concomitant risk assessment, should be a high priority for the secretary of defense.

2. EMPOWER A SENIOR DEPARTMENT LEADER FOR CYBER MATTERS, AND HOLD THAT PERSON ACCOUNTABLE.

If a problem arises such as one of the hypothetical scenarios above for which the Department of Defense bears responsibility, who is the responsible official? Recall the post-mortem discussion for the Zumwalt destroyer vignette. Because finger-pointing could continue for some time, the situation points to the need for a senior official responsible for the entire chain of events, and that responsibility demands significant empowerment.

We think that senior official should be an Under Secretary, recognizing that creating such a position requires congressional approval. Assuming that such an under secretary position was created, this official could also naturally become the principal cyber advisor established by Section 932 of the 2014 National Defense Authorization Act.

3. REDUCE THE DEPARTMENT'S INSATIABLE DEMAND FOR CYBER WORKFORCE TALENT.

It is almost universally agreed that the cyber workforce demand exceeds the supply of skilled workers. For example, Gen. John Hyten, commander of U.S. Strategic Command, recently opined that "[t]he [cyber workforce] demand signal is going to go nowhere but up and the capacity is not sufficient to meet all of the demand." Although this assessment acknowledges that the supply of skilled workers is currently insufficient, it does not explicitly recognize that capacity may never catch up.

This presents difficult choices for the Department of Defense because options for reducing the demand are elusive. Automation can (and surely must) help, and there are other risk-shifting approaches, such as requiring vendors to share some of the risk through product warranties, but these options cannot solve the full range of challenges. These and other alternatives for workforce demand reduction should be incorporated in concert with the risk assessment conducted as the department's set of cyber responsibilities is established.

While it may be tempting to draw the set of responsibilities narrowly, any solution that limits the department's responsibilities but fails to align them with its broad interests is short-sighted and ultimately self-defeating.

1. The author notes that American cybersecurity is not only a matter to be dealt with by the Department of Defense—which is who we usually think of when we think about warfare. What are some reasons you can think of for making more government agencies responsible for cybersecurity instead of centralizing it?

2. Cyberwarfare involves more than just harmless computer-to-computer attacks. As the author explains, weapons systems and military vehicles, among other things, are controlled by digital technology that could be victim to a cyberattack. What are some of the problems that can arise from this kind of connectivity?

CHAPTER 6

WHAT ORDINARY PEOPLE SAY

Everyone is talking about cybersecurity and cyberwarfare these days, from military veterans to politicians to everyday citizens. If you were to ask your friends and family about cyberwarfare, it's almost certain that every person you spoke to would have an opinion on the subject, and that no two opinions would be exactly the same. That's because everyone relies on the internet and the connectivity we all have to do at least something every single day. Your parents probably use the internet for work or to pay bills, your friends use Snapchat and Facebook to share their lives with you, your teachers buy school supplies online, and you have likely gone online to do your homework in the past few days. That means that everyone is vulnerable to a cyberattack—and that everyone is going to discuss what that means for them. This chapter will explore what different people think about cyberwarfare, and whether their opinions apply to a broader population.

"WHY NOW IS THE TIME TO ESTABLISH A STANDALONE CYBER FORCE," BY WELTON CHANG, FROM *TASK & PURPOSE*, APRIL 6, 2016

Does America need a cyber force? On one side of the debate is retired Adm. James Stavridis who analogizes the requirement to have a separate entity capable of operating in cyberspace to the creation of the U.S. Air Force. To Stavridis, the growing importance of cyberspace in future conflict is clear and the need for a cyber force obvious, and America can speed up adoption by bypassing the 20-year debate that surrounded the creation of the Air Force.

On the other side of the debate are the current heads of the Navy and Marine Corps, Adm. John Richardson and Gen. Robert Neller. Neither sees the need for a standalone cyber service. While the truth of the matter lies somewhere in the middle, it is probably closer to Stavridis' point of view. In the wake of the official Defense Department recognition of cyberspace as an operating environment, it is time to seriously consider standing up an independent cyber force.

Classic models of bureaucratic politics could have predicted these positions and without powerful advocates the likely outcome is no new force. A new cyber force would likely subsume current service cyber forces (e.g., Army Cyber Command, Marine Corps Forces Cyberspace Command). No service likes to lose resources and assets. Setting aside arguments rooted in bureaucratic infighting and jockeying, does the overall argument for an independent cyber service hold up?

CRITICAL PERSPECTIVES ON CYBERWARFARE

The main thrust of the pro-cyber force argument moves forward along two avenues: First, that cyberspace represents a distinct operating environment; and second, that in order to effectively operate in this domain, a separate and standardized set of skills needs to be developed, which are distinct from the sets of skills developed by existing services. In other words, warfare has changed so much that it necessitates a unified cyber capability.

Widespread convergence of physical and virtual realities, or the ability of the physical to be controlled via the virtual, seems to confirm this notion. Add in the amount of value in the world that exists mostly at a virtual plane — such as the billions of dollars of market cap in companies like Facebook and the amount of capital that flows through the world's banking systems that never existed as hard currency — and the notion of cyber being a separate domain seems uncontroversial. Manipulating matter in cyberspace, aside from physically destroying datastores and network communications lines, requires a skill set distinct from rifle marksmanship and driving an MRAP.

The follow-on question from the domain question is whether the military needs a separate and unified cyber force to effectively fight in cyberspace? Both separate and unified are important to this argument because one could envision the status quo going forward where each service has its own force (non-unified) with coordination occurring through U.S. Cyber Command. The notion of separate traditions, doctrine, equipment, and organization is a major part of the argument forwarded by the anti-cyber force camp. One issue that always comes up when depicting "cyber warriors" is of an out-of-shape hacker who refuses to wear a uniform.

While this seems to be a major preoccupation of the service chiefs (when asked about more lax physical and appearance standards, Neller refused to consider such possibilities), it doesn't necessarily follow that these "cyber warriors" all would fit this mold.

First, it is well established that exercise aids cognition. One need only look at exercise regimen of top video gamers and Silicon Valley programmers who are also obsessed with CrossFit to know that fitness and computing skill are not orthogonal concepts. Second, the entire argument about uniforms is a red herring designed to take attention away from the real issues. After all, what uniforms do special operations personnel wear while deployed? Clothes do not make people better at their job nor does it make them more professional. And if it really is a problem for recruits, they can always go and join the National Security Agency.

Beyond resourcing issues, the Navy and Marine Corps chiefs stated that coordination and integration would be impeded if cyber warriors were in their own service.

No doubt, integration and coordination are essential to proper employment of cyber capabilities. The "interagency" process is notorious for being an essential but ineffective part of Washington policy and war-making. However, this same line of argumentation, when taken to its logical conclusion, would also obviate the need for the entire Marine Corps because we already have the Army to fight on land and could also train the Army to do amphibious operations. A similar argument exists in favor of entirely subsuming the waterborne parts of the Marine Corps mission into the wider Navy. Coordination and integration are always hard, even within services.

So, on its own, the coordination argument doesn't hold much water.

Further dissecting the opposition, the question remains whether or not the additional coordination burden and resource expenditure is justified in terms of additional warfighting capability created. In other words, will housing all cyber forces under one roof create a net benefit? One important benefit would be the creation of unified training and skill standards for offensive cyber and network defense capabilities. Others include common operational language and standard procedures, programming language fluency, and uniform equipment base. Best practices, exploitations, and vulnerabilities can be rapidly shared, which is of utmost importance in a domain where information perishability and competitive advantages appear and disappear in minutes and seconds rather than days and years.

Ultimately the two sides are arguing past each other a bit. The issues regarding coordination are symptoms of long-recognized problems that arose with the last major reorganization of defense forces under the Goldwater-Nichols Act. By institutionalizing today's current structure of regional combatant commands, the advisory function of the Joint Chiefs, and relegation of the services to the role of "force provider," no service chiefs likely want to see further erosion of their responsibilities. In addition, the Goldwater-Nichols reorganization made sense in the age in which they were made, but today's world demands an overarching coordinating body for "whole-of-government" defense strategies. Even basic questions such as which DoD entity is in charge of civil assistance in the case of a domestic cyber emergency remains unsettled, according to a recent Government Accountability Office report.

Cyberspace, being everywhere (all pervasive), nowhere (owing to the replicability of data structures), and somewhere (servers and fiber exist in physical space), is not like the other domains. Organizations should adapt to environmental and technological changes or risk obsolescence. While the standup of a separate cyber force could be a massive waste of time and money without changes to the upstream command and control structure, it could also be a great net benefit to U.S. defense capabilities.

1. The author talks about how establishing a cyberwarfare unit would cost extra money, money that would come from taxpayers and from the other existing military forces. Do you think this is a valid consideration when it comes to cybersecurity issues?

2. If an organization is not up to competing on the cyber front, the author suggests they should be considered obsolete. Do you agree? What are some military or government groups you can think of that we don't need to be able to battle on the digital front?

CRITICAL PERSPECTIVES ON CYBERWARFARE

"CYBER WAR: REALITY OR HYPE?" BY CONN HALLINAN, FROM *FOREIGN POLICY IN FOCUS*, JANUARY 11, 2012

During his confirmation hearings this past June, U.S. Defense Secretary Leon Panetta warned the Senate, "The next Pearl Harbor we confront could very well be a cyber attack that cripples our grid, our security systems, our financial systems, our governmental systems." The use of Pearl Harbor provided powerful imagery: a mighty fleet reduced to smoking ruin, an expansionist Asian power at the nation's doorstep.

But is "cyber war" really a threat? Can cyber war actually "cripple" the United States? Or is the language just sturm und drang spun up by a coalition of major arms manufacturers, the Pentagon, and Internet security firms allied with China bashers aimed at launching a new Cold War in Asia?

The language is sobering. Former White House Security Aide Richard Clarke, author of Cyberwar, conjures up an apocalyptic future of U.S. cities paralyzed, subways crashing, planes "literally falling out of the sky," and thousands dead. Retired Admiral and Bush administration National Intelligence Director Mike McConnell grimly warns, "The United States is fighting a cyber war today and we are losing."

Much of this rhetoric is aimed at China. According to Rep. Mike Rogers (R-MI), chair of the House Intelligence Committee, the Chinese government has launched a "predatory" campaign of "cyber theft" that has reached an "intolerable level." Sen. Dianne Feinstein (D-CA) charges that a "significant portion" of "cyber attacks" on U.S. companies "emanate from China." Former CIA and National Security Agency director Michael Hayden told Congress, "I stand back in awe of the breadth, depth, sophistication, and persistence of the Chinese espionage effort against the United States of America."

China has been accused of hacking into the Pentagon, the International Monetary Fund, the French government, and the CIA, as well as stealing information from major U.S. arms maker Boeing and the Japanese firm Mitsubishi. The latter builds Japan's fleet of F-15s, the high-performance U.S. fighter jets.

The Pentagon has even developed a policy strategy that considers major cyber attacks to be acts of war, potentially triggering a military response. "If you shut down our power grid," one Defense official told the *Wall Street Journal*, "maybe we will put a missile down one of your smokestacks."

A FEEDING FRENZY

But consider the sources for all this scare talk: Clarke is the chair of a firm that consults on cyber security, and McConnell is the executive vice-president of defense contractor Booz Allen Hamilton. Both are currently doing business with the Pentagon.

Arms giants like Lockheed Martin, Raytheon, Northrop Grumman, Boeing, and other munitions manufactures are moving heavily into the cyber security market. In 2010, Boeing snapped up Argon ST and Narus, two cyber security firms with an estimated value of $2.4 billion. Raytheon bought Applied Signal Technology, General Dynamics absorbed Network Connectivity Solutions, and Britain's major arms firm, BAE, purchased Norkom and ETI.

"There is a feeding frenzy right now to provide products and services to meet the demands of governments, law enforcement, and the military," says Ron Deibert, director of the Canada Center for Global Security Studies.

There are big bucks at stake. Between the Defense Department and Homeland Security, the United States will spend some $10.5 billion for cyber security by 2015. The Pentagon's new Cyber Command is slated to have a staff of 10,000, and according to Northrop executive Kent Schneider, the market for cyber arms and security in the United States is $100 billion.

But is cyber war everything it's cracked up to be, and is the United States really so behind the curve in the scramble to develop cyber weapons?

According to investigative journalist Seymour Hersh, the potential for cyber mayhem has "been exaggerated," and the Defense Department and cyber security firms have blurred the line between cyber espionage and cyber war. The former is the kind of thing that goes on, day in and day out, among governments and industry, except its medium is the Internet. The latter is an attack on another country's ability to wage war, defend itself, or run its basic infrastructure.

Most experts say the end-of-the-world scenarios drawn up by people like Clarke are largely fiction. How could an enemy shut down the U.S. national power grid when there is no such thing? A cyber attack would have to disrupt more than 100 separate power systems throughout the nation to crash the U.S. grid.

Most financial institutions are also protected. The one example of a successful cyber attack in that area was an apparent North Korean cyber assault this past March on the

South Korean bank Nonghyup that crashed the institution's computers. But an investigation found that the bank had been extremely remiss in changing passwords and controlling access to its computers. According to Peter Sommer, author of the OECD report Reducing Systemic Cybersecurity Risk, the cyber threat to banks "is a bit of nonsense."

However, given that many Americans rely on computers, cell phones, smart devices, and the like, any hint that an "enemy" could disrupt access to those devices is likely to get attention. Throw in some scary scenarios and a cunning enemy—China—and it's pretty easy to make people nervous.

But contrary to McConnell's statement, the United States is more advanced in computers than other countries in the world, and the charge that the country is behind the curve sounds suspiciously like the "bomber gap" with the Russians in the 1950s and the "missile gap" in the 1960s. Both were illusions that had more to do with U.S. presidential elections and arms industry lobbying than anything in the real world.

AN ULTERIOR MOTIVE

The focus on the China threat certainly fits the Obama administration's recent "strategic pivot" toward Africa and Asia. China draws significant resources from Africa, including oil, gas, copper, and iron ore, and Beijing is beginning to reassert itself in South and East Asia.

The United States, meanwhile, now has a separate military command for Africa—AFRICOM—and the White House recently excluded U.S. military forces in the Asia theater from any cutbacks. Washington is also deploying U.S. Marines in Australia. As U.S. Secretary of State Hillary

Clinton told the National Defense University this past August, "We know we face some long-term challenges about how we are going to cope with what the rise of China means."

But James Lewis, an expert on Chinese cyber espionage, told Hersh that the Chinese have no intention of attacking U.S. financial services, since they own a considerable portion of them. According to Lewis, "current Chinese officials" told him "a cyber-war attack would do as much economic harm to us as to you." The United States is China's largest trading partner and Beijing holds over a trillion dollars in U.S. securities.

There is also a certain irony to the accusations aimed at China. According to *The New York Times*, the United States—and Israel—designed the "Stuxnet" virus that has infected some 30,000 computers in Iran and set back Teheran's nuclear program. The virus has also turned up in China, Pakistan, and Indonesia. In terms of cyber war, the United States is ahead of the curve, not behind.

What all this scare talk has done is allow the U.S. military to muscle its way into cyber security in a way that could potentially allow it to monitor virtually everything on the Internet, including personal computers and email. In fact, the military has resisted a push to ensure cyber security through the use of encryption because that would prevent the Pentagon from tapping into Internet traffic.

There is no question that China-based computers have hacked into a variety of governmental agencies and private companies (as have Russians, Israelis, Americans, French, Taiwanese, South Koreans—in short everyone spies on everyone), but few observers think that China has any intention of going to war with the much more powerful United States.

WHAT ORDINARY PEOPLE SAY

However, Beijing makes a handy bugaboo. One four-star admiral told Hersh that in arguing against budget cuts, the military "needs an enemy and it's settled on China." It would not be the first time that ploy was used.

If the Pentagon's push is successful, it could result in an almost total loss of privacy for most Americans, as well as the creation of a vast and expensive new security bureaucracy. Give a government the power to monitor the Internet, says Sommers, and it will do it. In this electronic field of dreams, if we build it, they will use it.

1. One of the arguments against better cybersecurity on the government side is the idea that if the government has that kind of power, they will use it against its citizens. Do you think this is a valid fear? Explain your reasoning using examples from other articles in this book.

2. The author says that cyberwarfare isn't as big a concern as it's made out to be, but the fact that everyone relies on their cellphones, tablets, and computers so much makes them more scared than they should be. Based on what you've read so far, do you agree? Use examples from this article and at least one other to support your answer.

"CYBER WARFARE: PREPPING FOR TOMORROW," BY BOBBY AKART, FROM *AMERICAN PREPPERS NETWORK*, OCTOBER 22, 2015

Albert Einstein once wrote:

I know not with what weapons World War III will be fought, but World War IV will be fought with sticks and stones.

In poll after poll, one of the primary threats concerning preppers is the use of a cyber attack to cause a collapse of our vulnerable critical infrastructure. There are many bad actors on the international stage – Russia, China, North Korea, Iran, Syria, and now the terrorist group, ISIS. Each is capable of wreaking havoc in the US by shutting down our power grid and enjoying the resulting chaos.

No bombs. No bullets. No swordfights. Just a few keystrokes on the computer.

And we're done.

Simply put, a Cyber Attack is a deliberate exploitation of computer systems. Cyber Attacks are used to gain access to information but can also be used to alter computer code, insert malware or take over the operations of a computer driven network.

Why would terrorists bother with an elaborate, dangerous physical operation—complete with all the recon and planning of a black ops mission — when they could achieve the same effect from the comfort of their home? An effective cyber attack could, if cleverly designed, produce a great deal of physical damage very quickly, and interconnections in digital operations would mean such an attack could bypass fail safes in the physical infrastructure that stop cascading failures.

One string of ones and zeroes could have a significant impact. If a computer hacker could command all the circuit breakers in a utility to open, the system will be overloaded. Power utility personnel sitting in the control room could do it. A proficient cyber-terrorist can do it as well. In fact, smart-grid technologies are more susceptible to common computer failures. New features added to make the system easily manageable might render it more vulnerable.

The very real threat posed to America by cyber warfare can be summarized by six central scenarios.

Over many decades, the U.S. has created the greatest military force the world has ever seen. But our research has proven that the biggest threat to national security comes from a computer with a simple Internet connection— not from aircraft carriers, tanks or drones.

THREATS TO THE PUBLIC SECTOR

The U.S. government fends off a staggering eighty thousand cyber attacks a year. There is good reason Director of National Intelligence James Clapper ranks cyber terrorism as the number one national security threat, ahead of traditional terrorism, espionage and weapons of mass destruction.

THREATS TO THE PRIVATE SECTOR

While rogue nation-states are interested in causing damage to governments, for some hackers and cyber criminals, cyber intrusions in the form of theft of intellectual property, personal data, and website defacement is enough to keep them occupied. The FBI notified nearly four thousand U.S. companies that they were the victims of cyber attacks in 2014. Victims of hackers ranged from the financial sector to major defense contractors to online retailers.

USE OF SOCIAL MEDIA TO ISSUE THREATS AND CALLS TO ACTION FOR TERRORISTS

Social media has become a haven for cyber criminals and terrorists. As Facebook, Twitter and Pinterest have become an integral part of our lives, criminals now use these venues to commit cyber theft or as a method of communication for terrorists. Nearly one in three U.S. adults say one of their social media accounts has been compromised. Cyber security analysts believe ten to fifteen percent of home computers globally are already infected with viruses and malware.

USE OF THE CYBER ARENA TO SPREAD PROPAGANDA TO GAIN ECONOMIC OR MILITARY ADVANTAGE

The Russians established a sophisticated propaganda machine under the supervision of its Internet Research Agency that waged a massive disinformation campaign in support for its annexation of Crimea and its invasion of Ukraine. These hired guns work hard, each one pumping out hundreds of comments and blog posts per shift. In addition, each hacktivist troll is reportedly required to post 50 news articles a day while maintaining half a dozen

Facebook and more than ten Twitter accounts. It is not unusual for this machine to be used to gain a militaristic advantage as the Russians spread incorrect information throughout the online media.

USE OF CYBER ATTACKS TO CONDUCT INDUSTRIAL ESPIONAGE

While the Russians are notorious for gaining a military advantage through the use of cyber tactics, the Chinese are a determined bunch when comes to stealing valuable public and private sector trade secrets. The vast majority of America's intellectual property theft is believed to originate from China. The Chinese employ elite hackers housed by the government throughout the world to mask their real affiliations. China's goal has been to catch up with the U.S. in direct military strength.

THE BIGGEST THREAT: COLLAPSE OF THE NATION'S POWER GRID

On July 8, 2015, Americans watched as trading was halted on the New York Stock Exchange (NYSE) floor. At the same time, computer reservation systems at United Airlines were down, and the *Wall Street Journal* newspaper computer networks crashed.

This was not a scene from your favorite author's books of fiction; it was very real. According to reports, the interruption of the services mentioned was a mere coincidence, and the events were unrelated. These incidents and many more have raised public awareness of the vulnerability of our nation's critical infrastructure.

HOW DO WE PREPARE?

Cybergeddon or World War C is not here yet, but it might be tomorrow. You never know when the day before—is the day before.

Under the most likely scenarios, the effects of a cyber war on most businesses are more likely to be disruptive than apocalyptic for two main reasons. Cyber intrusions can immobilize your business operations for hours and maybe days. Modern critical infrastructures tend to have enough built-in stop-gap measures and protections to prevent a cataclysmic crash of the entire power grid simultaneously or for an extended period.

However, the potential for a collapse of America's power grid is what concerns preppers the most. The threats we face are many. At FreedomPreppers.com, Americans are urged to prepare for a worst-case scenario. If nothing happens, you've lost nothing. For the United States, short of nuclear annihilation, the worst case scenario is an extended grid down collapse event.

Many preparedness consultants urge you to be ready for the plausible – natural disasters such as hurricanes, tornados, floods, earthquakes. At Freedom Preppers, we believe that a committed prepper is one who is ready for the worst-case-scenario, like a collapse of the critical infrastructure. Cyber Warfare is plausible, trust us. The extensive research we compiled can be found in our new book, *Cyber Warfare*, book one in the Prepping for Tomorrow Series. Once you have read this important analysis, I think you will agree that today is a great day to enhance your preparedness plan.

WHAT ORDINARY PEOPLE SAY

Because, we won't know from whom or from where, but we will certainly know when.

1. The author discusses how everyday Americans need to be prepared for the worst-case scenario when it comes to cyberwarfare. Based on what he says the dangers are, what are three ways you could prepare right now for a cyberattack?

2. One of the ways the average citizen can be harmed by cyberwarfare is through the spread of propaganda online. This was a hot topic in 2017 as Facebook announced that Russia had bought a number of political ads on its platform during the US presidential election in 2016. What are other ways bad actors can use the internet to spread propaganda?

"MORE CYBER PROFESSIONALS AT THE PENTAGON DOESN'T GUARANTEE BETTER SECURITY," BY WELTON CHANG, FROM *TASK & PURPOSE*, OCTOBER 20, 2015

It is not yet known if the recent U.S.–China agreement to limit cyber espionage is a meaningful step toward a more secure cyberspace. Without broader reaching, enforceable, and verifiable agreements coupled with a history of compliance, the Internet remains a near lawless and ungoverned battleground. Militaries around the world continue to stockpile cyber weapons and conduct reconnaissance on potential targets. The U.S. is no different and cyber is one of the highest priorities for the Defense Department: even in the age of austerity, U.S. Cyber Command's budget will double and personnel count will increase to 6,200. While some may laud the expansion of CYBERCOM and other U.S. government entities involved with cybersecurity, before we spend all of this money, we should pause and ask: Will all of these people and funding actually make us better at prosecuting cyber war and defending against cyber attacks?

Unfortunately, the fanciest security system in the world is useless if you don't lock your front door. All of the investment and talented personnel in the world won't be of much help if the U.S. government can't do the basic blocking and tackling such as data encryption and network authentication that is required for cyber defense. The seemingly numerous cyber security breaches, from the 23 million background investigation records exfiltrated during the Office of Personnel Management breach to reports that Russian hackers penetrated Joint Staff email systems, clearly indicates a systemic U.S. government failure to protect its information.

As long as individuals are susceptible to basic social engineering tactics, such as credential theft through "phishing," and federal agencies with sensitive information such as the IRS can't answer the simple question of how many servers are on their network, no amount of people or technology will make our networks safer. Adopting better cyber safety practices and making employees internalize them so they become second nature ensures we're crawling properly before attempting to walk in cyberspace. One thing is for certain, something must change and the current government standard of a yearly archaic half-hour "information awareness" training is just not enough to get people to truly practice safe cyber behavior.

Going beyond the basics, attracting talented programmers, developers, and cybersecurity professionals to work for the U.S. government, particularly the Defense Department, in any capacity has been a noted challenge. Even when new government professionals are brought into the system, the lure of moving to the private sector for double the salary and tech sector perks means that the proposed recruiting bump by the Defense Department is only a temporary band-aid on attrition.

But is this a story purely about incentives? Will paying government hackers and programmers handsomely stem the flow of boots out the door? The simple truth is that it will not. DoD and other agencies should focus less on trying to throw more people at the problem and instead focus more on ensuring that it utilizes and motivates its forces as efficiently as possible. For example, current thinking is mired in the antiquated concept that money is the be-all-end-all motivator; it is better to instead focus on the psychologically intrinsic aspects of motivation rather than the financial ones. Think of intrinsic motivation as three elements, autonomy, mastery, and purpose, according to Daniel Pink's summation of 40 years of psychological research. Putting purpose up front, service in defense of the nation, and giving these employees and service members the chance to grow under top-quality supervision is the best way to ensure that we have the best cyber corps going forward. This is something that private-sector jobs focused on financial gain simply do not address. How can building the next version of Farmville even compare? Naturally, there are limits to how far intrinsic motivation can go, so salaries should be at least seem "fair" after taking the patriotism discount. But if agency managers think that focusing on compensation will solve all of their problems, they are missing the motivational forest for the trees.

Another critical component that needs attention is making the military, federal and state governments smarter, faster, and more flexible in setting up personnel policies to make it easier for talent to get into needed positions of service, move laterally within government, and grow professionally. This is imperative as internet technology is pervasive and found across all aspects of government and unless cybersecurity talent is distributed across all agencies and organizations. The most comprehensive programs for recruitment and retention are concentrated at CYBERCOM and the NSA, which perpetuate "islands of cyber excellence" that could "leave non-security departments and agencies potentially vulnerable if they are unable to hire scarce talent," according to Peter Liebert, co-director of the Truman National Security Project cyber expert group and former DoD senior cyber policy analyst.

The U.S. government is moving forward; however, much more can be done. For example, the military

WHAT ORDINARY PEOPLE SAY

is only now enticing college students to sign up for cyber-specific ROTC initiatives, targeting a group that is increasingly graduating with enormous debt loads. New private sector outreach efforts like the new Silicon Valley office Defense Initiative Unit-Experimental are being extended to cities high in talented human capital and burgeoning tech sectors such as Austin, Pittsburgh, Baltimore, and Philadelphia. This gives DoD the ability to reach college grads with technical abilities who might otherwise have never considered military or government service.

Beefing up the Reserve and National Guard role in cyber defense is another promising plan that should be expanded to allow the military to tap into a technical base that represents the best of both worlds: private-sector opportunities and training while performing a mission vital to the nation's defense.

Finally, it isn't enough to focus on the tactical pursuit of line-level personnel, cyber is a strategic challenge as well. The utilization of cyber capabilities as a strategic tool is just as important as writing the latest hacking program. As P.W. Singer and Allan Friedman point out, existing cyber doctrine that emphasizes the superiority of offensive is inadequate because offensives can be both counterproductive and unpredictable and defense is not as weak as assumed. Thinking more clearly about the strategic and tactical use of cyber requires getting past the mantra of "offense rules" and also requires aligning recruitment goals. Right now recruitment is focused somewhat on quality but mostly on quantity. Unfortunately, a great hacker with technological creativity can outperform a thousand mediocre ones, because the mediocre ones will likely all arrive at similar conclusions while the standout ones will come up with novel solutions. The criticality of the internet to both daily life and defense operations mandates that we at least try to get the best people on board and have an employment strategy to match these talents.

1. The author notes that it's a challenge to lure talented cyber professionals to work for the government instead of Silicon Valley's big tech firms. What are some arguments you would make to a talented hacker to get them to consider working for the greater good instead of for personal gain?

"CHECK THE HYPE — THERE'S NO SUCH THING AS 'CYBER'," BY CHRIS ADAMS, FROM CHRIS.IMPROBABLE.ORG, MARCH 26, 2010

How can you tell the difference between a real report about online vulnerabilities and someone who is trying to scare you about the security of the internet because they have an agenda, such as landing lucrative, secret contracts from the government?

Here's a simple test: Count the number of times they use the adjective "cyber." Nobody uses the word "cyber" anymore, except people trying to scare you and trying to make the internet seem scary or foreign. (Think, for instance, of the term "cyberbullying," which is somehow much more crazy and new and in need of legislation than "online bullying.")

When was the last time you said, "I saw this really cool video in cyberspace" or "My cyber connection is really slow today"? Of course, no one speaks like that anymore. The internet is no longer distant or foreign (though it thankfully remains beautifully weird). It's familiar and daily. It's the internet. It's so ordinary, Wired.com stopped capitalizing it more than five years ago.

Need an adjective to describe something that is internet-based? Try "online."

But when it comes to scaring senators, presidents and the nation's citizens into believing the Chinese, the Russians or Al Qaeda are stealing all our secrets or bringing down the power grid, the internet somehow morphs back into "cyberspace."

Here's a good example of the "cyber" test from a pretty interesting story from *The Washington Post* about the National Security Agency disabling (rather ineptly, it seems) an online forum used by radical Islamic fundamentalists to plan terrorist attacks.

The Post uses the adjective 12 times in describing how the NSA and CIA bickered over whether NSA "cyber-warriors" should use hacking techniques to take down a message board that suspected Al Qaeda were using to make plans. In a brilliant stroke of "cyberwar," the NSA "cyber-operators" took down the CIA-sponsored honeypot message board where extremists were being monitored, somehow inflicting collateral damage on some 300 innocent servers in the process.

Forbes got into the "cyber" action this week as well.

Amit Yoran, a respected security expert who runs

a company that sells computer security services to the government, wrote a long post on a Forbes blog this week to defend the concept of "cyberwar," in no small part because this blog ranted about how that term is used to hype militarization of the internet and feed a new and very dangerous arms race.

Yoran says the debate doesn't matter (even as he falls firmly in the cyberwar camp), but what's important is that everyone recognize that the dangers of underestimating online risks is worse than "the impact of misrepresenting or miscalculating risk [...] in the sub-prime market," which led to "cascading global financial meltdown."

Gulp.

That sounds scary. Bad firewalls will lead to something worse than a global financial meltdown? (That sounds suspiciously like what Michael McConnell told President Bush to scare him into creating a secret government "cybersecurity" plan.)

Those looking for a reality check might check how many times Yoran uses "cyber" in the body of his piece?

The answer: 42. (Yes, we think that's funny, too.)

Yoran defines "cyberwar" as being launched via "cyber attacks" or "cyber exploitation." He defines the latter as "the compromise of these targets without their destruction or disruption, but rather through covert means, for the purposes of accessing information or modifying it or preparing such access for future use in exploitation or attack."

That's the very definition of what the NSA does — wiretapping abroad (and sometimes domestically), finding ways to spy on electronic machines simply by capturing their unintentional electromagnetic radiation, and scooping up radio and satellite communications of allies and adversaries alike.

Yoran and *Forbes* also fail to mention that his company, NetWitness, markets computer security equipment to the government and has a vested interest in the outcome of this debate.

Yoran disputes that his company stands to gain if the "cyberwar" terminology wins.

"We're not a government 'cyberwar' operation by any stretch and have nothing to gain by the terminology I suggested in my blog," Yoran wrote, saying that his company sells the exact same technology to corporations and governments. "I don't care what it's called. And think, if anything, the war implication is a bad one for many reasons."

But for those who relish the idea of a new front for war, it's way cooler and scarier to say we are in the midst of — and losing — a cyberwar, than to factually state that the Chinese want to steal our secrets and we want to steal theirs and we should have better computer security.

That kind of rhetoric doesn't launch sensationalist — and often demonstrably false — scare stories in opinion-making outlets like *60 Minutes, The New York Times, The Wall Street Journal, The Washington Post* and the *National Journal.*

No, when that kind of fear-mongering is needed to loosen the purse strings for computer security, only one word will do.

Cyber.

And it's even better when repeated ad nauseum in front of Congress and at the country's top security conferences by former and current government officials,

CRITICAL PERSPECTIVES ON CYBERWARFARE

even if those people couldn't even enable MAC address filtering on their own wireless routers.

Or as the Beastie Boys might have put it a couple of decades later, "Our Backs Are Up Against the Wall/Listen All Y'all, It's Cyberwar."

1. The author says that cyberwar isn't happening—mutual espionage is. However, he says, saying it's cyberwar sounds better to the people who want to rile up citizens. Based on everything you've read so far, do you agree with the author?

2. The National Security Agency has been accused of spying on citizens at home and abroad and also using digital tools to spy on other countries like China. Based on what you've read, does the NSA program that spied on regular American citizens seem more or less warranted than other forms of cyber security? Explain.

CONCLUSION

As you've now learned, cyberwarfare is as complicated as traditional warfare, though the stakes may at first seem much lower. But just because much of cyberwarfare takes place in the wires inside our computers and cellphones doesn't mean that it isn't serious—or seriously dangerous.

Cyberwarfare includes everything from computer and cellphone hacking to misuse of digital information to electronic weapons and drones. But it's a type of warfare not fought by armies, at least not traditional ones. The combatants in cyberwarfare can be intelligence operatives from foreign enemies like Russia or China, or they can be digital allies of the Islamic State here in the United States and Canada, or they can be everyday citizens—even ones who live down the street or work in your mom's office. Cyberwarfare has made it possible for anyone to attack those who they disagree with and want to harm, and it's much harder to defend against than people think. During a war, you can go into a bomb shelter or have an army protect you. During cyberwarfare, anyplace with an internet connection or cell signal is unsafe.

However, the United States and other countries around the world are trying to figure out how to keep citizens safe from cyberwarfare, even while they continue to seek ways to harm their enemies. As technology advances, we'll likely see both the protections available and the hurt that is possible increase, and it will be up to people like you to tell the government and the tech companies when enough is enough and when cyberspace needs to be free of war.

BIBLIOGRAPHY

Adams, Chris. "Check the Hype — There's No Such Thing As 'Cyber.'" *Chris.Improvable.org*, March 26, 2010. http://chris.improbable.org/2010/3/26/check-the-hype-theres-no-such-thing-as-cyber.

Akart, Bobby. "Cyber Warfare: Prepping for Tomorrow." *American Preppers Network*, October 22, 20115. http://americanpreppers-network.com/2015/10/cyber-warfare-prepping-tomorrow.html.

Alito, Justice Samuel A. Jr. *Spokeo, Inc. v. Robins*. United States Supreme Court, May 16, 2016. https://www.supremecourt.gov/opinions/15pdf/13-1339-new_4428.pdf.

Bossert, Thomas P. "Remarks by Homeland Security Advisor Thomas P. Bossert at Cyber Week 2017 — As Prepared for Delivery." The White House, June 26, 2017. https://www.whitehouse.gov/the-press-office/2017/06/26/remarks-homeland-security-advisor-thomas-p-bossert-cyber-week-2017

Buchanan, Bill. "If Two Countries Waged Cyber War on Each Another, Here's What to Expect." *The Conversation*, August 5, 2016. https://theconversation.com/if-two-countries-waged-cyber-war-on-each-another-heres-what-to-expect-63544.

Caldwell, Leslie R. "Rule 41 Changes Ensure a Judge May Consider Warrants for Certain Remote Searches." United States Department of Justice, June 20, 2016. https://www.justice.gov/archives/opa/blog/rule-41-changes-ensure-judge-may-consider-warrants-certain-remote-searches.

Cardozo, Nate. "D.C. Circuit Court Issues Dangerous Decision for Cybersecurity: Ethiopia is Free to Spy on Americans in Their Own Homes." Electronic Frontier Foundation, March 14, 2017. https://www.eff.org/deeplinks/2017/03/dc-circuit-court-issues-dangerous-decision-cybersecurity-ethiopia-free-spy.

Chang, Welton. "More Cyber Professionals At The Pentagon Doesn't Guarantee Better Security." *Task & Purpose*, October 20, 2015. http://taskandpurpose.com/more-cyber-professionals-at-the-pentagon-doesnt-guarantee-better-security.

Chang, Welton. "Why Now Is the Time to Establish a Standalone Cyber Force." *Task & Purpose,* April 6, 2016. http://taskandpurpose.com/now-time-establish-standalone-cyber-force.

Chatterjee, Bela Bonita. "Ready, Aim, Click: We Need New Laws to Govern Cyberwarfare." *The Conversation*, August 21, 2014. https://theconversation.com/ready-aim-click-we-need-new-laws-to-govern-cyberwarfare-30734.

Cilluffo, Frank J., and Sharon L. Cardash. "Russia's Aggressive Power is Resurgent, Online and Off." *The Conversation*, August

BIBLIOGRAPHY

25, 2016. https://theconversation.com/russias-aggressive-power-is-resurgent-online-and-off-64336.

Cox, Gregory V., and Priscilla E. Guthrie. "Getting 'Cyber' Right for the Department of Defense." *War on the Rocks*, November 9, 2017. https://warontherocks.com/2017/11/getting-cyber-right-for-the-department-of-defense.

Deane-McKenna, Conor. "The Next Cold War Has Already Begun — in Cyberspace." *The Conversation*, April 7, 2016. https://theconversation.com/the-next-cold-war-has-already-begun-in-cyberspace-57367.

Feffer, John. "North Korea: The Cyberwar of All against All." *Foreign Policy in Focus*, March 14, 2017. http://fpif.org/north-korea-the-cyberwar-of-all-against-all.

Forno, Richard. "How Vulnerable to Hacking is the US Election Cyber Infrastructure?" *The Conversation*, July 29, 2016. https://theconversation.com/how-vulnerable-to-hacking-is-the-us-election-cyber-infrastructure-63241.

Forsling, Carl. "Should Cyber Warfare Have Its Own Branch?" *Task & Purpose*, June 28, 2016. http://taskandpurpose.com/cyber-warfare-branch.

Glance, David. "Claims of US Hacking of China Levels the Moral Ground — What Next for the Cyber War?" *The Conversation*, June 15, 2013. https://theconversation.com/claims-of-us-hacking-of-china-levels-the-moral-ground-what-next-for-the-cyber-war-15223.

Hallinan, Conn. "Cyber War: Reality or Hype?" *Foreign Policy* in Focus, January 11, 2012. http://fpif.org/cyber_war_reality_or_hype.

Keller, Jared. "An Anonymous Hacker May Have Compromised John Kelly's Cell Phone. It's Only a Sign of Things to Come." *Task & Purpose*, October 6, 2017. http://taskandpurpose.com/john-kelly-phone-hack-compromised.

Kersley, Esther, Alberto Muti, and Katherine Tajer. "The Cooling Wars of Cyber Space in a Remote Era." *Common Dreams*, November 7, 2014. https://www.commondreams.org/views/2014/11/07/cooling-wars-cyber-space-remote-era.

Moore, Daniel. "Struggling with Cyber: A Critical Look at Waging War Online." *War on the Rocks*, July 5, 2017. https://warontherocks.com/2017/07/struggling-with-cyber-a-critical-look-at-waging-war-online.

Obama, Barack. "Remarks by the President at the Cybersecurity and Consumer Protection Summit." The White House

Archives, February 13, 2015. https://obamawhitehouse.archives.gov/the-press-office/2015/02/13/remarks-president-cybersecurity-and-consumer-protection-summit.

Obama, Barack. "Remarks by the President on Securing Our Nation's Cyber Infrastructure." The White House Archives, May 29, 2009. https://obamawhitehouse.archives.gov/the-press-office/remarks-president-securing-our-nations-cyber-infrastructure.

Prince, Daniel, and Mark Lacy. "In Cyber-War, You Could Change History at the Touch of a Button." *The Conversation*, March 6, 2014. https://theconversation.com/in-cyber-war-you-could-change-history-at-the-touch-of-a-button-23324.

Rosenzweig, Paul. "Cyberwar is Here to Stay." *The Conversation*, February 24, 2016. https://theconversation.com/cyberwar-is-here-to-stay-54938.

Sear, Tom. "Cyber Attacks Ten Years On: From Disruption to Disinformation." *The Conversation*, April 26, 2017. https://theconversation.com/cyber-attacks-ten-years-on-from-disruption-to-disinformation-75773.

Shackelford, Scott. "Is It Time for a Cyber Peace Corps?" *The Conversation*, October 25, 2017. https://theconversation.com/is-it-time-for-a-cyber-peace-corps-85721.

Trump, Donald. "Presidential Executive Order on Strengthening the Cybersecurity of Federal Networks and Critical Infrastructure." The White House, May 11, 2017. https://www.whitehouse.gov/the-press-office/2017/05/11/presidential-executive-order-strengthening-cybersecurity-federal.

Vanaskie, Thomas I. *United States of America v. Apple MacPro Computer, et al*. United States Court of Appeals for the Third Circuit, September 7, 2016. http://www2.ca3.uscourts.gov/opinarch/153537p.pdf.

Zook, Michelle Villarreal. "How Should the US Respond to Cyber Attacks?" *Task & Purpose*, January 13, 2015. http://taskandpurpose.com/u-s-respond-cyber-attacks.

CHAPTER NOTES

CHAPTER 3: WHAT THE COURTS SAY

EXCERPT FROM *SPOKEO, INC. V. ROBINS*, FROM THE UNITED STATES SUPREME COURT, MAY 16, 2016

1. The Act defines the term "consumer report" as: "any written, oral, or other communication of any information by a consumer reporting agency bearing on a consumer's credit worthiness, credit standing, credit capacity, character, general reputation, personal characteristics, or mode of living which is used or expected to be used or collected in whole or in part for the purpose of serving as a factor in establishing the consumer's eligibility for—
   "(A) credit or insurance to be used primarily for personal, family, orhousehold purposes;
   "(B) employment purposes; or
   "(C) any other purpose authorized under section 1681b of this title."
15 U. S. C. §1681a(d)(1).

2. "The term 'consumer reporting agency' means any person which, for monetary fees, dues, or on a cooperative nonprofit basis, regularly engages in whole or in part in the practice of assembling or evaluating consumer credit information or other information on consumers for the purpose of furnishing consumer reports to third parties, and which uses any means or facility of interstate commerce for the purpose of preparing or furnishing consumer reports." §1681a(f).

3. This statutory provision uses the term "consumer," but that term is defined to mean "an individual." §1681a(c).

4. For purposes of this opinion, we assume that Spokeo is a consumer reporting agency.

5 See Edwards v. First American Corp., 610 F. 3d 514 (CA9 2010), cert. granted sub nom. First American Financial Corp. v. Edwards, 564 U. S. 1018 (2011) , cert. dism'd as improvidently granted, 567 U. S. ___ (2012) (per curiam).

6. "That a suit may be a class action . . . adds nothing to the question of standing, for even named plaintiffs who represent a class 'must allege and show that they personally have been injured, not that injury has been suffered by other, unidentified members of the class to which they belong.'" Simon v. Eastern Ky. Welfare Rights Organization, 426 U. S. 26, 40, n. 20 (1976) (quoting Warth, 422 U. S., at 502).

7. The fact that an injury may be suffered by a large number of people does not of itself make that injury a nonjusticiable generalized grievance. The victims' injuries from a mass tort, for example, are widely shared, to be sure, but each individual suffers a particularized harm.

8. We express no view about any other types of false information that may merit similar treatment. We leave that issue for the Ninth Circuit to consider on remand.

EXCERPT FROM *UNITED STATES OF AMERICA V. APPLE MACPRO COMPUTER, ET AL.*, BY JUDGE THOMAS I. VANASKIE, FROM THE UNITED STATES COURT OF APPEALS FOR THE THIRD CIRCUIT, SEPTEMBER 7, 2016

1. Encryption technology allows a person to transform plain, understandable information into unreadable letters, numbers, or symbols using a fixed formula or process. Only those who possess a corresponding "key" can return the information into its original form, i.e. decrypt that information. Encrypted information remains on the device in which it is stored, but exists only in its transformed, unintelligible format. Although encryption may be used to hide illegal material, it also assists individuals and businesses in lawfully safeguarding the privacy and security of information. Many new devices include encryption tools as standard features, and many federal and state laws either require or encourage encryption to protect sensitive information.

2. According to the affidavit submitted in support of the federal Government's search warrant application, "cp" stands for

CHAPTER NOTES

"child pornography" and "pthc" stands for "'pre-teen hard core." (App. 39.)

3. A "hash" is "[a] mathematical algorithm that calculates a unique value for a given set of data, similar to a digital fingerprint, representing the binary content of the data to assist in subsequently ensuring that data has not been modified." The Sedona Conference Glossary for E-Discovery and Digital Information Management 21 (Cheryl B. Harris, et al. eds., 4th ed. 2014). Hash values are commonly used in child pornography investigations. *See, e.g., United States v. Ross*, 837 F.3d 85, 87 (1st Cir. 2014); *United States v. Ackerman*, 831 F.3d 1292, 1294 (10th Cir. 2016); *United States v. Thomas*, 788 F.3d 345, 348 n. 5 (2nd Cir. 2015); *United States v. Brown*, 701 F.3d 120, 122 (4th Cir. 2012); *United States v. Cunningham*, 694 F.3d 372, 376 (3d Cir. 2012; *United States v. Cartier*, 543 F.3d 442, 444-45 (8th Cir. 2008).

4. *United States v. Doe* does not dispute the validity of the underlying search warrant issued by a Magistrate Judge under Fed. R. Crim. P. 41.

5. There are, of course, instances when a contempt proceeding may be the only avenue for challenging the underlying order to produce information. For example, judicial review of a grand jury subpoena may be obtained only by refusal to comply with the subpoena, with the validity of the subpoena being litigated in the ensuing contempt proceeding. *See, e.g., United States v. Ryan*, 402 U.S. 530, 532-33 (1971) ("[W]e have consistently held that the necessity for expedition in the administration of the criminal Rylander, 460 U.S. 752, 756 (1983) (quoting *Maggio v. Zeitz*, 333 U.S. 56, 69 (1948)); In *re Contemporary Apparel, Inc.*, 488 F.2d 794, 798 (3d Cir. 1973) (same). Furthermore, Doe did not argue in the District Court that the Decryption Order was not an appropriate exercise of authority under the All Writs Act. Thus, even if the propriety of the Decryption Order was before us, our review would be limited to plain error. *Brightwell*, 637 F.3d at 193. Under this framework, an appellant must show four elements: "(1) there is an 'error'; (2) the error is 'clear or obvious, rather than subject to reasonable dispute'; (3) the error 'affected the appellant's substantial rights, which in the ordinary case means' it 'affected the outcome of the district court proceedings'; and (4) 'the error seriously affect[s] the fairness, integrity or public reputation of judicial proceedings.'" *United States v. Marcus*, 560

U.S. 258, 262 (2010) (quoting *Puckett v. United States*, 556 U.S. 129, 135 (2009)). In *New York Telephone*, the district court had issued an order authorizing federal agents to install pen registers in two telephones and directed the New York Telephone Company law justifies putting one who seeks to resist the production [to a grand jury] of desired information to a choice between compliance with a trial court's order to produce prior to any review of that order, and resistance to that order with the concomitant possibility of an adjudication of contempt if his claims are rejected on appeal."); In *re Grand Jury Subpoena*, 709 F.3d 1027, 1029 (10th Cir. 2013)("A protesting [grand jury] witness may seek appellate review only after he refuses to obey the subpoena and is held in contempt.").

6. In its Order explaining the contempt ruling, the District Judge observed that Doe had failed to object to the Magistrate Judge's determination that Doe's Fifth Amendment rights were not violated by the Decryption Order despite being warned that such failure "may constitute a waiver of appellate rights." (App. at 15 (citing *United States v. Polishan*, 336 F.3d 234, 240 (3d Cir. 2003).) Thus, the District Court did not address the Fifth Amendment issue.

7. It is important to note that we are not concluding that the Government's knowledge of the content of the devices is necessarily the correct focus of the "foregone conclusion" inquiry in the context of a compelled decryption order. Instead, a very sound argument can be made that the foregone conclusion doctrine properly focuses on whether the Government already knows the testimony that is implicit in the act of production. In this case, the fact known to the government that is implicit in the act of providing the password for the devices is "I, John Doe, know the password for these devices." Based upon the testimony presented at the contempt proceeding, that fact is a foregone conclusion. However, because our review is limited to plain error, and no plain error was committed by the District Court in finding that the Government established that the contents of the encrypted hard drives are known to it, we need not decide here that the inquiry can be limited to the question of whether Doe's knowledge of the password itself is sufficient to support application of the foregone conclusion doctrine.

GLOSSARY

cyberattack—Any attack that occurs online; it can include someone hacking into a computer to spy on another party, or stealing information from another person's or government's computer.

cyber Command—Also known as USCYBERCOM, this is a subordinate agency to the National Security Agency and is responsible for assisting the Department of Defense with all cyber operations and cybersecurity issues.

cybersecurity—The issue of protecting online access and documents; cybersecurity can include things like protecting your computer from being hacked, to making sure you have strong online passwords. For the US government, it means protecting government computer networks from being hacked.

cyberspace—The online world, or the internet.

cyberwarfare—Fighting between two major entities—generally governments from opposing countries—that takes place online. It involves things like wrongfully accessing another country's computer network, or interfering with that country's ability to get online or network with other computers in its system.

Department of Defense (DoD)—The government department responsible for all warfare and the military. The DoD is also responsible, with Cyber Command, for protecting the country from, and waging, cyberwar.

Department of Justice (DoJ)—The government department responsible for how courts and law enforcement agencies operate.

digital—Anything that happens on a computer, tablet, or smartphone is digital, taking place only on a screen and not physically tangible.

espionage—Spying.

National Security Agency (NSA)—A national intelligence agency under the Department of Defense. Much of the work done by the NSA involves cybersecurity and cyberwarfare.

CRITICAL PERSPECTIVES ON CYBERWARFARE

Pentagon—The building where the Department of Defense is housed; often used interchangeably with DoD.

prepper—Someone who believes there is immediate danger of a large-scale cyber attack or war and who believes it is important to be prepared for the worst-case scenario. Preppers are known for stockpiling food and other items in case of an emergency.

PRISM—A program run by the National Security Agency that collects data from major telecommunications companies; the program is often used to suggest that the US government spies on American citizens.

propaganda—Advertising material that strongly pushes a political agenda.

sovereignty—Freedom and self-governance, particularly of a country.

FOR MORE INFORMATION

BOOKS

Brooks, Rosa. *How Everything Became War and the Military Became Everything: Tales from the Pentagon*. New York, NY: Simon & Schuster, 2016.

Chapple, Mike, and David Seidl. *Cyberwarfare: Information Operations in a Connected World*. Burlington, MA: Jones & Bartlett Learning, 2014.

Goodman, Marc. *Future Crimes: Inside the Digital Underground and the Battle for Our Connected World*. New York, NY: Anchor Books, 2015.

Hayden, Michael V. *Playing to the Edge: American Intelligence in the Age of Terror*. New York, NY: Penguin Press, 2016.

Kaplan, Fred. *Dark Territory: The Secret History of Cyber War*. New York, NY: Simon & Schuster, 2016.

Klimburg, Alexander. *The Darkening Web: The War for Cyberspace*. New York, NY: Penguin Press, 2017.

Perkovich, George, and Ariel E. Levite, ed. *Understanding Cyber Conflict: 14 Analogies*. Washington, DC: Georgetown University Press, 2017.

Powers, Shawn M., and Michael Jablonski. *The Real Cyber War: The Political Economy of Internet Freedom*. Chicago, IL: University of Illinois Press, 2015.

Singer, P.W., and Allan Friedman. *Cybersecurity and Cyberwar: What Everyone Needs to Know*. New York, NY: Oxford University Press, 2014.

Valeriano, Brandon, and Ryan C. Maness. *Cyber War Versus Cyber Realities: Cyber Conflict in the International System*. New York, NY: Oxford University Press, 2015.

WEBSITES

The Rand Corporation
www.rand.org/topics/cyber-warfare
This nonprofit think tank works with the Department of Defense and other government agencies on matters of national security.

Task & Purpose
www.taskandpurpose.com
Task & Purpose is a military news website that features writing by veterans and active-duty service members who have expertise in matters of combat and national security.

War on the Rocks
www.warontherocks.com
This news and analysis website is focused on military and defense issues, including cyberwarfare.

INDEX

A
Amazon, 29
AmeriCorps, 17–19

B
Bossert, Thomas, 67–75
bots, 138
Bronze Night, 139
Budapest Convention, 149
Bush, George W., 43, 162, 188, 206

C
Carter, Ash, 171
CENTCOM, 157
China, 10, 16, 31, 35, 37–38, 57, 70, 137, 147, 149, 157–159, 164–168, 170–172, 188–189, 191–194, 197, 199, 205–209
Churchill, Winston, 45
CIA, 94, 189, 205
Clapper, James, 39, 134, 195
Clinton, Hillary, 39, 47, 155, 192
Cohen William, 22
Cold War, 6, 13–14, 20, 47, 133, 135, 167, 170, 172, 188
Conficker, 96
Consumer Privacy Bill of Rights, 62
CrowdStrike, 36
cybercide, 27–28, 30
CYBERCOM, 200, 202, 217
Cyber Command, 9, 183, 184, 190, 200
Cyber National Guard, 19
cyber-vandalism, 27

D
DARPA, 155
DDoS (denial of service) attack, 14–15, 22–25, 27–28, 35, 138–140, 159–160
Democratic National Committee, 35, 39, 46, 133
Department of Defense, 11, 61, 74, 85, 133, 154–156, 173–181, 183, 186, 188–190, 192–193, 199, 200–203
Department of Homeland Security, 22, 81, 118
Department of Justice, 112, 114
Digital Millennium Copyright Act, 51
DNS server, 24–25

E
elections, 6, 20, 39, 46, 48–53, 94, 112, 133, 153, 162, 173–174, 191, 199
electronic voting, 48–52
Estonia, 15, 25, 27–29, 35, 137–139, 141–142, 147, 149
Ethiopia, 143–145

F
Fair Credit Reporting Act of 1970 (FRCA), 103–106
FBI, 46, 74, 94, 196
Fifth Amendment, 117, 119, 122, 125–129
First Amendment, 152
FinSpy, 144
Foreign Sovereign Immunities Act (FSIA), 143, 145
Fourth Amendment, 114

G
Geneva Conventions, 163
Goldwater-Nichols Act, 186
Gulf War, 137

H
Hobbes, Thomas, 161

I
India, 19, 28–29
infrastructure, 14, 16, 22, 24–26, 28, 36, 38, 41, 46, 57, 59, 71–72, 74, 76, 78, 82–84, 92, 96–97, 99, 134, 139, 141, 147, 154, 163, 167, 174–175, 190, 194–195, 197–198
intellectual property, 37, 58, 70, 95, 165, 196–197
International Humanitarian Law, 44
Islamic State, 31, 34, 68, 157, 170, 176, 194, 209

K
Kelly, John, 153–156, 211

L
Lynn, William, 10

M
malware, 11, 14, 40, 49, 60, 69, 93, 95, 116, 143–145, 158, 162, 164, 176–177, 194, 196
McCain, John, 174
movies, 6–8, 31, 162

N
National Crime Agency, 25

221

National Security Agency (NSA), 145, 166, 185–189, 202, 205–206, 208
National Security Council, 96–97
NATO, 32, 35, 139, 154
New York Stock Exchange (NYSE), 94, 197
Nitro Zeus, 9, 12
North Korea, 6–7, 40, 58, 70, 75, 137, 158–159, 161–165, 190, 194
nuclear weapons, 9, 14–15, 68, 162

O
Obama, Barack, 9, 11–12, 55–66, 92–101, 155, 163–166, 168, 191
Office of Personnel Management, 38, 88, 200

P
passwords, 63, 118–120, 129–131, 191
Peace Corps, 17–21
People's Liberation Army, 37
power grids, 9, 12–13, 17, 22, 26, 36, 57, 93, 95, 133, 159–160, 170, 188–190, 194–195, 197–198, 205
preppers, 194, 198
PRISM, 145, 166–167
privacy, 57, 59, 60–66, 71, 77, 86, 93, 97–98, 100, 132, 193
propaganda, 196, 199
Putin, Vladimir, 46

R
Rapuano, Kenneth, 144–145

Red Cross, 44
Rule 41, 114–116, 123
Russia, 6, 9–10, 13, 15, 20, 28, 31, 35–36, 38–40, 46–47, 57, 70, 96, 133–140, 149–150, 153–155, 157–159, 162, 170, 172, 191–192, 194, 196–197, 199–200, 205, 209

S
Secret Service, 94, 166
Security Operations Command, 150
Silicon Valley, 94, 185, 203–204
Snowden, Edward, 145, 166–168
social media, 10, 24, 47, 57, 100, 136–137, 157, 177, 182, 184, 196–197, 199
Sony, 6, 7, 40, 58, 64, 67, 70, 157–159, 162
Spokeo, Inc. v. Robins, 103–113
spyware, 60, 93, 144, 163
Student Digital Privacy Act, 62
Stuxnet, 15–16, 147, 170, 192
SWIFT network, 40
Syria, 6, 15, 29, 174, 194

T
Tallinn Manual, 28, 35, 138–139, 149
Target, 159
terrorism, 13, 47, 57, 61–62, 64, 79, 82–89, 92, 95–96, 164–166, 194–196, 205
THAAD missile, 163
Trump, Donald, 46–47, 67–7, 72, 74, 76, 91, 153, 155, 162–164
  executive order, 76–91

U
Ukraine, 9–10, 13–17, 36–37, 133, 135, 140, 154–155, 159, 196
urbicide, 27–28
United Nations (UN), 72, 159, 163
United States v. Apple Macpro Computer, 117–130

V
Victory Day, 138
viruses, 60, 70, 144, 158, 170, 192, 196

W
World War II, 45, 138

X
Xi Jinping, 165

ABOUT THE EDITOR

Jennifer Peters is a writer and editor whose work has focused on everything from relationships to books to military and defense issues. During her more than ten years working in the media, her work has appeared in a number of magazines and online news and culture sites, with her most recent bylines appearing on *VICE News* and *Task & Purpose*. She lives in Washington, DC, and she never leaves home without a good book.